# MAKE ME FALL

## Bayshore #2

## Ember Leigh

Make Me Fall © 2019 by Ember Leigh

All rights reserved.

No part of this book may be reproduced in any form or by any electronic or mechanical means, including information storage and retrieval systems, without written permission from the author, except for the use of brief quotations in a book review.

This book is a piece of fiction. Names, characters, places, and incidents are the products of the author's imagination or are used fictitiously. Any resemblance to actual events, locales, or persons, living or dead, is coincidental.

This book is licensed for your personal enjoyment only.

This book may not be re-sold or given away to other people. If you are reading this book and did not purchase it, or it was not purchased for your use only, then you should return it to the seller and purchase your own copy. Thank you for respecting the author's work.

Published by Ember Leigh, 2019

EmberLeighAuthor@gmail.com

Cover art: Covers by Combs

Editing: Elisabeth R. Nelson

Proofreading: Leona Bushman

# ABOUT 'MAKE ME FALL'

**There's one rule in my family:** *stay away from the Daly brothers.*

We were raised to know them as users. Manipulators. But I only ever saw Connor as the enigmatic senior hottie who dropped into fifth period to teach us about the perils of drunk driving.

So when my first big girl job out of college ends up with us working at the same company, it's heart throb city all over again. Except he's way ahead of the game. Successful, talented, put together. I'm just a frumpy twenty-something in a quarter life crisis who doesn't know a glue stick from a makeup highlighter.

He would never want me, even though he's all I ever wanted in secret. So when we cross paths one night at the bar and one drink leads to another, he slaps me with an offer I can't refuse.

Accompany him back to Bayshore, flight included.

Only stipulation? Pose as his girlfriend.

Our families will flip, but I'm not strong enough to say no to those baby blues, especially if it means I'll have a chance to spend the next two weeks with my adolescent heart throb.

We've got two weeks to prove we're head over heels for each other.

Which is just enough time to make me fall.

# contents

# CHAPTER ONE

KINSLEY

"Are you kidding me? I'm gonna need to see some ID."

The warning bark of the bartender makes me grit my teeth. He's acting like I'm a sixteen-year-old sneaking into the bar to inhale shots of RumChata.

But he's got it all wrong. I'm a twenty-five-year-old who is legally seeking shots of RumChata, because I've earned it after my work week.

"Here, hang on." I fumble with my purse, which also looks like something a sixteen-year-old might buy while posing as an adult. It was from a thrift store near my apartment, which specializes in forgotten goods from the eighties. The overly large pearl snap pops free and shoots across the bar like a fifty-cent firework.

I get carded a lot, so you'd think I'd be used to having to prove my baby face. But no. Today, I'm fucking over it.

My license won't come out of the hardened plastic cover of my snap wallet, which also has an entire section available for checks. I don't carry checks, so instead I shove interesting business cards in the flap. One flutters out—a funny sex shop I stumbled across recently, *Spankin' Trails*. I look like a total mess, and I know it.

"Look." I shove the whole wallet his way, and he peers at it like he's never seen a license in his life.

"Fakes are getting pretty good these days," he mumbles, then pushes it back my way. "You don't look a day over twelve."

I huff and roll my eyes. "Come on. I might look young, but I'm not prepubescent, for God's sake. So come on. RumChata, buddy."

He side-eyes me while he stomps off to prepare my drink, like he's trying to figure out my game. This is no game. This is one hundred percent Kinsley: stumbling, gangly, baby-faced Kinsley.

I sigh and relax into the high-backed barstool. I came here for one express purpose—to forget the hell that is my job—but now, I can't get past the hell that is my life outside of work.

I've been on the west coast for almost eight years. Since I left Bayshore at age eighteen to study at UCLA, I've been cultivating the Californian side of my Ohio-based DNA. And really, things started out great. College was wild and fun. I got a degree. I found an amazing job. But then...things went south. Like all the way down to Antarctica south.

My dream job turned into professional purgatory. My apartment rent skyrocketed, because #SanDiego. And then I realized that all my peers were maturing in some other universe. My contoured contemporaries look like gorgeous aliens compared to my plain, un-mascara'd Midwestern features. I don't know how to catch up, and more importantly, I'm not sure if I want to. And more than that, the only man I ever dared to date turned out to be only a touch more stable than the type of men you might see on those true crime shows.

How can I be twenty-five and already as lost as an octogenarian with an iPhone? All the inspirational memes imploring me to *Live*

*Truthfully* and *Be Your Authentic Self* just piss me off. How can I be truthful and authentic *and* make my rent?

I guess this is what they call the quarter-life crisis.

*Great.*

Voices murmur quietly around me in this lounge. It's the closest bar to my workplace, and I've been here a few times before. Never with Burly the Bartender though. He must be new. This is the type of fancy place which has wood floors and mirrors along the walls. So everyone can see how rich and powerful they are while sipping the sweet nectars that distract us from our terrible jobs.

If this isn't the definition of #adulting, I don't know what is.

Burly finally comes back with my RumChata—*thankyouverymuch*—and I sip quietly, finally feeling some of the tension leaving my shoulders. Ahh, this is the life. Coaxing myself into forgetfulness about my stifling boss before I go home, alone, to my overpriced apartment and lack of social life.

One of the nearby tables, a cluster of businessmen, breaks up with a flurry of platitudes and good-natured shoulder clapping. They were here when I came in, and as they disperse, one of the biz bros catches my eye.

He's broad-shouldered, and even his gray button-down can't hide the fact that he's built beneath his clothes. A dimpled grin steals my breath as he turns my way.

I know this face.

He's Connor Daly. That blond and toned hunk who works at the same company as me. One of the infamous Daly brothers from back home. The man who the sixteen-year-old drinking RumChata inside of me is suddenly squealing over.

Instead of leaving with the rest of his business squad, Connor heads for the bar. The smile drops from his chiseled jaw, and something raw pours out of him. He probably doesn't notice me spying. I blend into anything eighties themed, as well as most lounge spaces.

I can't pry my gaze off him as he slides onto a barstool about five seats down from me. The bartender serves him immediately, no crap given about his age, and pretty soon, Connor has three shots lined up in front of him.

Now, I'm really curious. Connor has always been the golden boy, even back in our school days. I didn't see him all the time, since he was a grade ahead of me, but it's as true now as it was then. Back in the days when I fawned over him, it was because he delivered good-natured lectures about not drinking and driving. And now, I fawn over him because he's one of the top developers at our company.

He tosses back a shot. And then another. After the third one is downed, I can't resist the urge to know more. I pick up my hard-sided purse and shuffle his way.

He doesn't seem to notice me. Which is whatever. Nobody really does anymore. Not since college. It's the theme of my adulthood—no longer a girl, but somehow not a woman. I don't know what the secret code is that all females received, but the package never showed up at my door, despite being promised two-day delivery.

I clear my throat as I settle into my spot and flag down the bartender. He shows up a moment later.

"Another RumChata, please." I pause, glancing over at Connor. "And whatever he had there, two more of those."

Connor snorts, and his unfocused gaze swings my way. He has the same electric blue eyes as the rest of his brothers, which is the sort of blue that will land most people a modeling deal in these parts. It's almost painful to meet his gaze. His handsomeness is foreboding. Like he's going to break my heart, and I don't know it yet. Even though that's impossible.

Connor would never be with someone like me.

How do I know this? Because he's with my boss. And that evil witch is my opposite. So, thanks to math, we know scientifically, he is incapable of being with someone like me.

"Are you buying me another shot?" he asks, and the tang of rum reaches me. I shrug.

"Seems like you're lamenting something. I am too. Why not lament together?"

My heart is racing. God, it's hard work to sound casual. But maybe this is the start of my new journey as a real woman. Striking up conversations at the bar with my disgruntled colleague and former heartthrob. I'm pretty sure Connor and I haven't exchanged more than thirty words in our lifetime, but that doesn't matter. I'm here to push that count up to forty.

Connor heaves a long, drawn out sigh. "My grandma died."

I wince. "Oh, shit. I'm really sorry to hear that." I pinch the bridge of my nose, trying to search out her name in my memory banks. I don't know much about the Dalys, other than the following: all of the brothers are stupidly hot; and all of the brothers are stupidly off-limits.

My parents got into it with Connor's parents a billion years ago, and nobody has gotten over it. I grew up knowing the Dalys were a bad bunch without ever really knowing *why*. But that doesn't matter to me. We're in San Diego. My parents won't see me unless I accidentally FaceTime, which I've actually done during a make-out session before. I'll fraternize with the devil if I want to. Especially if he's built like an Abercrombie model turned software nerd.

"She had dementia really bad," Connor says, and he sounds choked, fighting emotion. I frown, scooting closer to him. I resist the urge to sling my arm over his shoulders.

"That's the worst," I offer. "Did you just find out?"

He shakes his head. "At work earlier, but I had this meeting right after."

"Ah. So it's still...fresh."

Burly returns with our shots, and I push one immediately over to Connor. I lift mine in the air, gesturing it toward him as if to ask, *Ready?* He nods and picks it up.

Then his gaze swings up to meet mine. Electricity doesn't just spark, it damn near fries my bones to dust. My forearms go hot, and I wonder if he felt that too. Or maybe this is my teenaged unrequited love acting up again.

We take the shots with a grimace. Once he slams the glass to the bar top, he clutches at the front of his hair.

"I have to go back to Bayshore."

I nod, studying the dark blond hairs at his neckline. "I haven't been there in ages," I say.

What does the man look like under this business-casual attire? I've caught his shirt unbuttoned down to the third button on two occasions, but usually it's unbuttoned two down. Not that I keep track of this in a spreadsheet. *Anymore*, I mean.

He blinks a few times, and then, he's watching me again. Something churns behind those eyes, but I can't meet his gaze long enough to figure it out.

He snorts, and then he reaches out, wrapping an arm around my shoulders. He brings me into him, like a side hug.

"My Bayshore buddy," he croons. He squeezes my shoulder again, which sends heat tiptoeing between my legs. I want to pretend this is a romantic grab, but it's not. He's jostling me like he's greeting a frat brother after years apart.

I laugh nervously, and he leans in, his eyes sparkling.

When he opens his mouth to speak, the blunt rum force reaches me before his words. "You should come with me."

# CHAPTER TWO

CONNOR

Listen, I'm drunk.

But that doesn't mean I don't know what I'm doing.

I know *exactly* what I'm doing. I'm sitting in this bar, sad as fuck because my grandma died, and fighting back bitterness with a bat as my drunk mind hovers over the thing I don't really want to think about, which is that I've been an idiot for the past six months.

My being an idiot has nothing to do with my grammy, by the way. She's lovely. Was lovely. Fuck, the past tense thing is going to get me. Having to stave off dealing with it for an entire day means that it's burbling up like one of those baking soda volcanoes from middle school. It's spilling everywhere and making a mess. Sure, the rum didn't help. But that's what coping mechanisms are for: helping in the worst way possible.

Rum + Grammy = This ridiculous proposition I made.

I don't even know this girl's name. I just know that we spent twelve years of school under the same roof, and now by some weird stroke of luck, we work in the same company on the opposite side of the country from where we grew up. What are the chances? I normally know her name—I really do. But tonight, the rum has taken it from me.

"Listen," I say, when her eyes grow saucer wide. I'm not slurring, so I don't know why she's looking at me like she can't understand me. "It's good to go back to Bayshore every once in a while."

Her brows furrow deeper. "I don't have the money to go home right now, honestly."

Here's the thing about my ridiculous proposition. It's not just ridiculous, it's also desperate. But she doesn't need to know that.

"For what, flights?"

She nods. "I got a new car. Well, a used car. A new-to-me sort of car. I don't really have anything left over for a plane ticket."

My gaze wanders over her while she nibbles at her lip and fidgets with the napkin beneath her glass. She's got glossy strawberry blonde hair, the stuff of surf magazines. It's pulled back into an exceptionally long braid, one so long that I can't help but pick up the tip of it. I hold it out from her body, inspecting the length of it.

"What is this, three feet long?"

She shrinks a little. "Two feet, actually."

I flick the tip back and forth over my thumb, and she buries her mouth in her palm. Like maybe she's enjoying this. My mind goes stupid places—braid tips as erogenous zones—and I snort.

"What?"

"Nothing." I drop the long plait, facing her more fully in my chair. She stays facing the bar top, but the creep of a blush in her cheek tells me she's more than aware of my attention.

I've never looked at her this much. Never spoken to her even half as much. She's the type of girl who sticks to the shadows, whether from being overlooked or choosing to stay there herself. In a word, she's unremarkable. High-waisted pants, a very modest blouse. I can't tell if she's A-shaped, pear-shaped, or no-shaped underneath her clothes. Her black loafers are uninspiring. She leaves everything to the imagination, without even a whiff to go on.

"So you don't want to come back to Bayshore with me?"

I'm not going to forget. She doesn't know it yet, but she's the perfect girl for a position that was recently vacated. My ex can-barely-call-her-a-girlfriend was originally on hand for shit like this. But we finally ended it last week, after way too many months of a back and forth that damn near gave me motion sickness.

I thought we'd been compatible—good looking twenty-some-things, and desperate for success. Even the appearances of it. But apparently there's more to compatibility than that.

Still, my brothers are going to be in Bayshore too. My mom and dad will be expecting the platinum-encased report of my life out west. Dom and Grayson, in particular, are going to be waiting to hear of any perceived stumble so that they can gloat about how much more successful they are.

Well, I don't make as much money as them. Nowhere near it. And the only trump card in my euchre hand right now is the fact that I'll be the only one with a girlfriend. Which was true up until very recently.

I just want to make it true again, for the length of my time in Bayshore.

"I mean, I'd *like* to go home, sure—"

"I'll buy your ticket."

She narrows her eyes with a look that says, *come on.* "You're not buying my ticket."

"Why not? I've got the money."

"But you—" She sputters a little. "We don't even—"

I lean forward, and my fingers brush her wrist. She clamps her mouth shut, and her gaze falls to her hand.

"We're Bayshore buddies." I squeeze her wrist gently, and she bites her bottom lip. "We're from the same place. That means something. We've got a bond that nobody else has because of it."

I'm that level of drunk where I will spew any bullshit necessary to get what I need. And I can tell this homely little lass will eat it up. She's got eyes the color of a summer sky bordered with periwinkle, and there's something sharp and hot in her gaze that makes my forearms prickle. I can't tell if she's naïve or just one of those conscious virgins.

"A bond, huh?" Her voice is husky in her disbelief, and something in her laugh makes my memory spark. *Kinsley.* That's her name. I remember it because Tamara always made fun of her for it. She called it manly. Tamara, my ex-barely. Tamara, Kinsley's boss.

Tamara had a problem with Kinsley from day one, and I only half listened to her complaints. I have enough of my own work drama that I don't usually have the energy to get enmeshed in someone else's. But that's the other perfect dimension to this arrangement.

Tamara will lose her shit if I take Kinsley back to Bayshore with me.

And if there's one juicy revenge I have an appetite for, it's that.

"Kinsley. When's the last time you went back?" I ask, scooting my chair closer.

She's nibbling on her bottom lip again. "It's been a few years..."

"Too long. *Way* too long. Let me treat you. Come on. I'm going anyway, and I could use the company on the plane."

She's tugging at the damp bits of the napkin beneath her glass. "When would you leave?"

"In a few days. I haven't even looked at flights yet."

"And for how long?"

"Probably two weeks."

She shakes her head. "I can't take a two-week vacation like that. That requires planning. I—"

"Do you have any pets?"

She frowns. "No."

"Any plants? Succulents? Out-of-control vines?"

A smile ghosts her lips. "No, none of that."

"Then you'll be fine. Our company is permissive with personal days. If you can use a few of those and rack up the vacation days on the backend, you're golden."

She sighs, drumming her fingers against the bar like she's really thinking about it. "It would be nice to see my parents again."

"Let me make it happen for you."

She rubs at her face, lets out a little squeal into her palms, and then shouts, "Okay! This is crazy, but I'll do it."

I squeeze her shoulder, but this time, I notice the feminine curves beneath her silky shirt. The narrow width of her shoulder blade, which begs for a slouchy shirt or the slipping strap of lingerie. Heat prickles through me, but I know this is the alcohol speaking. Kinsley and I, we don't run in the same circles. It's the type of truth that simmers on the backburner, always burbling and true.

Which makes my next proposition even more outrageous, but all the more doable.

"It's important to get home once in a while." I send her my best winning smile. Even more important than getting home is proving to my family that I live up to their absurd standards of achievement. Especially my overbearing father, who has made my life a particular kind of hell since the day I turned twelve and officially joined the "compete-o-sphere."

That hardened battle ring where my two older brothers and I spar with frequency, urged on by the ringleader: Dad.

"I just wonder if you could do me one small favor." I try to keep my voice light. Casual, even. Like I'm not about to ask the most absurd thing ever. "I need you to pose as my girlfriend while we're home."

She blinks a few times, and her hesitant blue eyes find mine for a split second. Serious question marks brew there, a witch's cauldron of confusion. "What?"

"I know it sounds crazy," I insist, and that's when I notice my slur. Shit. Not helping my case. "It would really help me out. My family...they..."

"Why wouldn't you take your girlfriend?"

I stare at her dumbly for a moment, getting lost in the delicate planes of her face. Freckles splash across her cheeks, and she's got a sun kissed quality that makes her look younger than she probably is. I know we went to school together, so it's impossible that she's the eighteen years old that she honestly looks. I'm twenty-seven, so it's impossible for her to be *that* young.

"Tamara?" she prompts, when I've remained silent too long.

"Oh," I blurt. "Right. Well, she's not my girlfriend. That's why I'm not taking her." My chest tightens slightly, but not because I miss her. Tamara and I had the Urban Dictionary definition of a toxic relationship. Laden with foul language and street terms to describe how poorly we fit together. Because sometimes, Webster's just doesn't quite capture it.

"But haven't you guys been together forever?" Kinsley asks.

"We broke up a while ago," I tell her. And if you count the moment I emotionally disengaged from her, it was even longer. I knew from the beginning it was a bad choice, but that's part of what makes me an idiot. I was hanging on for something she'd promised to deliver. So who's fault is it when she didn't come through?

Hint: mine.

Kinsley softens. She turns the empty tumbler of RumChata back and forth in her hands. Every cell in my body is tight with anticipation. *Just say yes.* If she goes along with this, I will give her so much more than a plane ticket to see her family. I will construct a shrine in her likeness and kiss its feet on the daily. Because she's helping me complete the trifecta.

Get back at Tamara, prove to my family I'm better than I actually am, and last but not least, piss off my dad.

Because Kinsley isn't just any ol' Bayshore buddy. Oh no. She's Kinsley *Cabana*. The daughter of my mom's ex-best friend and dad's most hated enemy in the world.

Sure, I want to look good compared to my brothers. But what's a competition without ruffling some feathers?

Bringing Kinsley home isn't just going to ruffle them. It's going to burn them to a crisp.

The rum made me a genius, and I would kick myself tomorrow if I didn't at least try when presented with this unexpectedly perfect opportunity.

"You're drunk," she accuses, but I can see the alcohol glow in her own eyes.

"So are you."

"No, I'm tipsy," she says, right as she wobbles off the stool. She catches herself on the lip of the bar and giggles.

"Come with me," I urge, reaching for her wrist again.

And maybe that's what does it. The heat of her tan skin under my hand causes my fingers to close around that delicate wrist, and my thumb strokes a lazy pattern over her pulse. I catch a barely audible gasp.

"Right now?" she asks, voice barely above a whisper.

Her naivete makes me smile. God, she's cute, for how oblivious she is. "To Bayshore," I clarify.

"Oh, right." She straightens, reaching for her purse. "Give me your number, and I'll sleep on it."

I'm putting my number into her phone before she can say otherwise. When the check comes, I pay for everything, even her rounds of RumChata from earlier.

"We'll have fun." I get one last glimpse of those pretty eyes before I leave the bar.

Inviting Kinsley to accompany me back home wasn't on my agenda. But even though she hasn't made up her mind, I can already see the shifting shadows of the coming days with her at my side.

There's something in that strawberry blonde braid that promises adventure.

I just wonder if I'm prepared for it.

# CHAPTER THREE

KINSLEY

I barely sleep that night. How could I? Connor touched my wrist *three separate times* in the most overt display of chaste flirtation since the dawn of Victorian romance novels.

And yeah, I masturbate. Because how could I not?

How can I even with this man?

It's not difficult to push myself over the edge, writhing on the bed with my fingers between my legs, imagining how much further things could have gone. In an alternate universe, surely, because despite the fact that he wants me to pose as his girlfriend, I'm not dumb enough to think that it means we'll actually *do things*.

Even though I would give several fingers from my non-dominant hand for a chance to have Connor rub himself against me. Hell, I would settle for seeing the outline of his cock, not even fully hard, through some boxer briefs. And in my wildest fantasies, I see him sliding two fingers over the damp crease of pussy, pushing aside my underwear...before slipping them ever-so-slowly inside...

I don't even need to imagine actual sex with the man for me to orgasm. That's how bad I've got it for him.

Connor is my dream man, but only from afar. I know nothing about him, so I'm not silly enough to think we'd be a perfect match. But from the outside? He's a broad wall of masculinity, easygoing grins tempered with studious looks that make him run his thumb along his square jaw. I've caught him in meetings before, and he trains those blue eyes on the speaker with so much intensity, I'm surprised they don't burst into flames.

And after our brief encounter at the bar, I can taste his intensity like a fine wine. It's hard not to get drunk on it. Hell, I wanted to say yes from the get-go. Embarrassment kept me from signing on the dotted line. Because how silly is that? Am I *that* starved for affection that I'll jump at the first chance to play pretend girlfriend with my high school heartthrob?

The answer isn't just *yes*. It's *hell yes*.

My ex—whose name I no longer pronounce in an effort to banish him from my heart space like a very misbehaved dragon—left me wrecked. He didn't only lower my self-esteem, he completely deflated it. That's not why I have ugly purses, mind you. No, I carry these outdated monstrosities because I *want to*.

One sleepless night later, I am convinced of what I must do. I'm already emailing Tamara my sudden and desperate request for personal days, followed by the formal application for vacation days through the HR system. I remind my boss of my redundancy, which I already know she'll bring up. Honestly, I welcome the break from that bitch.

Tamara is a fearsome woman, though I'm not sure which is scarier—her too-perfectly manicured claws, or the way she brandishes her emotional reactions like weapons in the office.

I want her job, because I could do it better. More fairly. I graduated with a business administration degree from UCLA three years ago, and I thought I'd be further up the ranks in the Human Resources world by now.

But Tamara has kept me under her thumb, flooding me with bitch work and unsavory training modules which make me think she hates me.

Tamara is everything I am not. She is the living embodiment of an HR poster imploring employees to report workplace abuse: wide, toothy grin framed by perfectly mauve lipstick. Mahogany hair never out of place, not even a strand. She's tall and sexy yet somehow modest. She seems like she has it all together. And for a while she even had Connor, meaning she also had it all.

So how do I report workplace abuse if the person I report it to is the one perpetrating the abuse?

I could start a job hunt, but the thought depresses me. Isn't this what I was gunning for? I fought to be on the West Coast, and now I don't know what I'm doing wrong. I just know that something isn't right. Tamara plays a part as much as my lack of promotion and sad, nonexistent social life does. Why go out when I'd rather Facetime my college buddies while we share boxed wine in different cities? We have episodes of *Friends* to catch up on, which is a tradition we started ironically once we parted ways after UCLA.

Dating is out of the question, too. I already know that I'm too frumpy to live, and all the dating apps I've tried end up with an avalanche of underwhelming dick pics. Besides, my ex did me in. The first man I dated out of college was borderline emotionally abusive—though I guess being borderline abusive just makes someone *actually abusive*. He thought I was beautiful one day and a Cinderella-style wretch the next. He never failed to tell me, either—to build me up so he could tear me back down. I withstood it for a year. And now, a year later, I feel like I'm finally crawling out of the cave he left me in.

So maybe this little jaunt to Bayshore is what I need. Connor couldn't have known how right he was. I'm hopeful the visit back home to Mom and Dad will jostle me out of this funk. Maybe the lake air will give me clarity that the hustle and bustle has been drowning out.

I text Connor at nine a.m., once I finally accept I won't be sleeping anymore, no matter how hard I try.

*KINSLEY: OK. I'm in. Let's do it.*

He doesn't reply for so long, I'm afraid that it really was a drunk offer he never intended on following through with. I let ten minutes tick by in agonizing indecision.

*KINSLEY: Unless you were drunk and kidding?*

When my phone finally dings with a response, my entire body goes rigid. I'm grimacing before I even look at the screen. I'm fully prepared for extreme disappointment. The offer was too good to be true. He slept off the alcohol and woke up regretting it. Here it comes.

*CONNOR: Hope you requested off the dates already bc I got our tickets. Leaving Tuesday. Fwding confirmation now.*

My work email inbox dings next, and I can barely believe my eyes as I watch the airline confirmation materialize before my eyes.

Holy shit.

This is really happening.

I'm going home with Connor for two full weeks...posing as his girlfriend.

Excitement churns hot and wild inside me. I whoop with excitement as I roll out of bed. This means I've got three days to get packed and presentable. I'll need new shoes. And a couple new tops, probably. An emergency thrift store run is in order.

Just because it's all for show doesn't mean I don't want to actually impress him.

Connor is a free agent. Which means that if even a slice of my wildest dreams comes true, this trip back to Bayshore will be the best trip ever.

# CHAPTER FOUR

CONNOR

We agreed to meet at the airport check-in. I'm business premium, so I'm checked in and ready before I even get to the airport. Which means I'm pacing the entry hall waiting for Kinsley while I compulsively check my phone.

Traveling is not my favorite thing. In concept, sure, it's great. But being trapped in cars and planes for long periods of time drives me nuts. Usually within an hour or two, I'm ready to bounce off the walls. Having somebody with me is also a logistical move. The distraction helps me tolerate the tedium.

But when Kinsley shows up carrying an olive-green duffel bag like she's trying to get cast for a bad remake of a war movie, I realize I might have made the wrong choice. This girl is not normal. In the sober light of day, I can't remember why the hell I thought asking a stranger to pose as my girlfriend was wise.

Yes, this will piss off my dad. Yes, I will appear to have succeeded in the relationship department. And yes, Tamara will absolutely have a conniption once she finds out Kinsley and I are "together." But I forgot one crucial detail in my evil scheme.

I have to spend the next two weeks with this person.

*What the fuck was I thinking?*

Kinsley looks flustered as she hobbles up to me. I hurry to take the duffel bag out of her hands; it feels as though she's packed fifty-pound dumbbells, exclusively. I grunt as I haul it over my shoulder. My abs engage, and I stumble slightly.

"What the hell is in here?"

"Well, hello to you too." She smiles sheepishly, pushing back some flyways from her blonde braid. "Just the essentials, you know? My jet-setting essentials."

I snort. "Which includes steel beams and iron dumbbells, right?"

"Oh, come on. It's not that heavy. I carried it in fine."

"You were limping."

She breezes past me. "I need to check in."

I follow her to the next open gate agent, who processes her ID and prompts her to put her bag on the scale. The red number ticks upward until it finally lands at fifty-three. The gate agent narrows her eyes and tuts.

"This bag is over the allowable weight limit," she says in a mechanized voice. "You'll have to reduce it or pay an overage fee."

Kinsley swears and opens the bag right there. She starts rummaging through the contents. Over her shoulder, I can see she's packed about a billion books. Of course it's so damn heavy.

"You know they have books in Ohio too," I whisper. She shoots me a look and then pulls out her selections, which she stuffs into her oversized purse. The luggage still registers too heavy, though, so to end this painful episode, I offer to pay the overage.

"You really don't have to," Kinsley says. "I can take out some more books—"

"We need to get to the gate. Just let me pay."

She stares at the bag, tapping her finger against the countertop. "I'll pay you back."

"How about you lend me a book instead?"

A dimply grin crosses her face, and the shyness in her smile prompts a smile on my own face. If this had been Tamara, I would have found makeup weighing down her bags. The woman packed an arsenal large enough to paint the faces of a thousand Fashion Week models. I pay the employee, and a conveyor belt carries Kinsley's bag into the bowels of the airport. We make our way through security and into the current of people traversing the concourse.

Nervousness rolls off her. It's in the way she keeps fiddling with the gold chain around her neck and smoothing down the front of her gray slacks. She's dressed like this is a business trip but is nervous like we're going to pull off a heist. Once we reach the gate and pick some seats on the outer edge, I bring up the thing we've been avoiding all along.

"So. Let's talk about...the rules, I guess?"

She nods vehemently. "Yes. Just tell me what I need to do."

"I don't want this to be weird or uncomfortable. My old room has two separate twin beds, so it's not like we have to share a bed or anything. We'll act like a couple, minimal PDA required. Maybe holding hands or a kiss on the cheek would be the extent of the affection. Does that sound doable?"

"Totally." She flashes a smile, hazarding a glance at me. She doesn't meet my gaze much, and I find myself staring at her and searching out a glimpse of those periwinkle eyes. "Do you want me to tell my parents we're dating too?"

"No, we only want my family to know." I lean back in my seat, crossing my ankle over my knee. "Do you think they'll be suspicious if you're staying at my house?"

She shrugs. "I told them I'm staying at a friend's house."

An announcement informs us priority boarding is beginning. That's us. We shuffle into the line and take our seats in the middle of business class. Kinsley coos as she settles into her seat, straightening her legs out in front of her.

"I can actually extend my leg all the way."

"Luxury, right?"

She inspects the area around the arm rests and discovers the USB ports. "Oh, lord. I can charge my phone, too? This is VIP." She twists around, scanning the aisle. "Where are the warm towels and welcome champagne?"

"It's just business class. They only wipe your ass like that in first class."

She snickers. "Then I demand an upgrade."

"You're in business class for five minutes and already need more." I tut. "I've ruined you."

"You have." She nudges me as an attendant files past. "Ask her if she'll do the ass wiping."

A laugh bursts out of me. I don't think I ever said the words *ass* and *wipe* next to each other around Tamara. She probably would have puked into her hand. Something about Kinsley makes me a little looser than normal. Maybe it's the grandma pants or the total lack of feminine pretension that she carries around with her. I can't imagine kissing her, even though she has a great mouth, with perfectly plump lips.

The thought shudders through me. What would kissing her be like?

I look past her out the window, focusing on the tarmac below. Thoughts like those should be avoided. I'm 90 percent not attracted to Kinsley. Well, maybe 80 percent. I can still remember just how slight her shoulder felt when I touched it at the bar the other night. And yeah, I kinda got hard from that. At any rate, her ears stick out from her head too much. We could never be together.

The plane finishes loading, and when we're up in the air, I feel the usual restlessness setting in. Kinsley is already buried in a book, and the way she's furrowing her brow, I don't want to interrupt her. My mom is a bookworm, and I know what happens when you annoy an avid reader.

I pull out my briefcase and open my laptop. This is the best way to channel my energy: puzzling over software code. I've been working on a new app for almost six months, something I started because Tamara said she had an in with a competing company that would pay me more, if only I could present a solid app in my portfolio.

But not just any company. WeGo, which is the newest Google competitor to emerge on the scene in the past year. The place is apparently as innovative as Apple, with plans to become as ubiquitous as Amazon. But getting in is hard. Like *Mission Impossible*-style hard, with Tom Cruise rappelling past the laser beams and all. You either need to know somebody or already *be* somebody.

And it turns out, I know someone.

Tamara.

Except I hate thinking that I've been working on this shit for six months only to lose my chance at this prestigious opportunity. Snagging this job would be a boon to my resume and probably make me a software wunderkind if I can finagle it. She knows the HR department there and had promised to get me in as a favor. But now that we've parted ways, I'm not counting on her being nice for the hell of it.

But I should finish the app anyway and use it to scout myself a better job. WeGo might be off the radar for now, but that doesn't mean I can't find a better gig elsewhere. Because I'm sick of going nowhere in this company. I'm sick of being one of the top developers only to be retained in my department because I'm the most efficient. I want more money; I want more control. Right now, I'm a talented, speedy grunt worker, churning out code for the coupon empire I work for.

"I thought you were on vacation."

Kinsley's voice makes me jolt. I turn to her, pulling out the ear buds that weren't playing anything. It's a force of habit from big city life. "I am."

"Then why are you coding?"

"This isn't for work." I roll my shoulders. I'd been hunching and tense—standard coding position. I pull off the black-rimmed glasses I use when I stare at my laptop for hours on end and rub my eyes.

"Is this what your leisure time looks like?"

I heft with a laugh and lean back in the seat. "Maybe?"

"Well, as your fake girlfriend, I really don't think it's healthy for you to be coding during our vacation," she says in a mock-serious tone. "Especially as we've been fake planning this for months and months. You never fake pay attention to me anymore."

The way she's looking at me is so tongue-in-cheek serious that I can't even keep a straight face. A laugh ripples out of me, but I squash it.

"Sorry, sweetie." I close my laptop, turning toward her with a shit-eating grin. Faking this type of argument is probably the type of practice we need. She's a smart cookie. Way smarter than I bargained for. Maybe Tamara didn't get her quite right after all. "How can I fake make it up to you?"

She stumbles at that, blinking up at me with doe eyes that betray some level of innocence that blurs the line between pretend and reality.

But Kinsley recovers quickly. She slaps down a little booklet onto her tray table: *1001 Crossword Puzzles.* "Help me do this puzzle."

She couldn't have known it, but this sudden crossword puzzle feels like a breath of fresh air. At the very least, it will kill an hour of an otherwise frustratingly long flight. And that is as good as gold.

I might have done something right after all in picking Kinsley to accompany me.

I just hope that proves to be the case when we land in Ohio.

# CHAPTER FIVE



We glide into the Cleveland airport with enough time to make it to Bayshore for dinner. The closer we get to Bayshore, the flatter the land. Familiar sights snag my attention—the fireworks billboard on Route 2 that still says "Have a bangin' time"; the particular cluster of trees and marshland that signals the fact that we're *almost home.*

It's been two years since I've set foot in Bayshore, and all of it has to do with money. San Diego isn't cheap, and though I make enough money at my job, all of it goes to just keeping afloat. A better car, a replacement washer, even an unexpected mole removal that set me back about five hundred dollars. If that isn't the mark of adulthood, I don't know what is. Washers and mole removals. I really thought adult life would be more exciting than this.

As it is, this spur-of-the-moment trip to Bayshore is the most exciting thing that's happened in a *long* time. Yes, going back to my hometown is the travel highlight of my mid-twenties. Though I have to admit having Connor at my side is a type of fantasy fulfillment I never saw coming. The sight of him in my periphery alone is enough to make me internally fangirl.

I don't know what it is about him. Yes, he's quick witted and handsome and roughly six foot perfect. But I think what keeps me in constant melt mode is the fact that I used to pine for him so hard back in high school. Ever since he came into my sixth period geometry class to interrupt the teacher with a trifold presentation about drunk driving, I've been a hopeless victim of his blond-hunk good looks. Even back then, he had some sort of golden surf-boy quality that has only been further polished by his time on the west coast.

But more than that, the feud between our parents lent him an enigmatic untouchability. Like he, along with all the rest of his brothers, was some type of exotic jungle fruit which nobody was really sure was poisonous. My sisters didn't share the same fascination, so I always kept it to myself. I made sure my squiggly renditions of Connor's name stayed in the margins of my school notebooks only.

And now that we're adults, I'm sure everyone will be fine with the fact that we're showing up together. So much time has gone by. Who even cares anymore? It's something I repeat to myself as Connor merges onto the offramp leading into Bayshore. The words turn into a mantra as we cruise into town and head for his parents' house.

Once we're parked in the lakeside neighborhood, staring at the backs of unfamiliar SUV's and a brand-new VW, panic cinches my chest.

"Your parents aren't going to, like...*care* that I'm here, right?" I ask. This whole idea seemed so much easier and non-problematic when we were two thousand miles west. When staying at his parent's house in Bayshore was still a *concept*.

He sends me a flat look. "They'll be fine. We're all adults."

True. We're all adults. But you can't really count on adulthood for much. Aside from mole removals and new washers, we're all just barely mature children. I want to tell Connor this—*remember how our parents have hated each other for three decades? They're technically adults too*—but he's pushing out of the car. He comes around toward the stone path as the front door swings open.

His mother Annette is there, a family-portrait-worthy smile on her face.

I shut the passenger door, facing the front porch. A submissive smile plastered on my own face. The one that says, *Hi, I'm no trouble at all. Will you let me in the house?*

Annette's gaze moves past Connor and lands on me. Her smile evaporates, like water on summer asphalt.

No trace of it anywhere. Fucking gone.

I can only stare as Connor approaches her and wraps her in a hug. She hugs him back, and I step forward carefully, as one would around a pregnant cat. I'm not here to cause problems. I'm here to be Connor's girlfriend for the next two weeks. No drama, please.

Connor sweeps his arm toward me. He's talking, but I can't hear over my sudden and crippling anxiety. His mother's razor gaze slices over me.

"Kinley and I have been together for a while," Connor is saying as I step up to him. He wraps his arm around me, pulling me into him.

"Kinsley," Annette says, less like a greeting and more like a test. "Cabana."

"That's me." I offer another one of those ultra-sugary smiles, and my arm slingshots around Connor's waist. He is my anchor in this terrifying maternal sea, and I'm not letting go. "Great to see you again. It's been a long time."

And it has. I ran into her in the Daily Shop a few times during my teens; I saw her at school functions, notably the senior musical presentation of *Annie*, in which Connor acted as President Roosevelt. And yes, I only went to the musical to see Connor.

She inhales deeply, her eyes fluttering slightly, as if she's drawing a cleansing breath from the bowels of the earth. A tight grin graces her narrow face.

"Time for dinner," she says, in the pinched tone which only a super pissed-off mom can manage.

Once Annette stomps inside the house, I turn to Connor and fist his button-down at the front of his chest. "What have you gotten me into?" I hiss.

"It's fine," he reassures me, the heat of his arm still securely draped over my shoulders. God, it feels good. It really does. Even though I'm slightly worried I'll be poached inside the Daly household like a trophy animal. Something to send home to my parents; the ultimate victory. *Ha ha! We've got your daughter! Now, make them break up, or she's dead!*

"That didn't feel *fine*," I whisper as we step into the house. It's cozy and updated, with white trim, wood floors, and driftwood-style frames around pictures of lakes. I swear, that's some sort of obligation in my hometown—every inhabitant of Bayshore must display at least three pictures showcasing #lakelife, or they'll be forced out of the town.

"Do you need to drop off your bags, honey?" Annette's voice drifts from further inside the house. "Connor," she adds, in case I thought that *honey* was directed at me. Connor drops his arm from around my shoulders, pauses, then grabs my hand. He gives me a deeply meaningful look. The type of look that makes my ovaries clench from *needing to bear his children.*

"We're going to meet my dad now." His voice has the tone of an executioner. Inevitably fatal.

"Okay," I say, but before I can get my bearings, Connor is leading me deeper into the house, and then *bam*, we're facing the entire Daly clan. Annette flits between kitchen and dining room, while the big oak table is surrounded by the guys. All of them. Starting with the burly and formidable Mr. Daly, and Connor's four brothers.

Holy hell, I forgot what it was like to be around the Daly boys. The Daly *men*. Because whatever I remember from high school is way, way outdated now. These guys have matured and in the best way possible. But Connor still blows the rest of them away. They might be a family of hotties, but Connor is the Babraham Lincoln to rule them all.

The conversation quickly dies down, and all eyes are on us. Mr. Daly clears his throat.

"Hey, fam," Connor says, the start of a shit-eating grin on his face. "Long time no see. I brought my girlfriend. You guys remember Kinsley Cabana?"

"Jesus Christ." Mr. Daly massages his forehead for a moment, his eyes closing. His jaw works back and forth. He's salt and pepper at the temples, but his dark brown hair is still as vibrant as his sons'. All of them except Connor, that is.

Grayson, the second eldest, stands suddenly, waving us toward the table. "Connor, don't keep her over there like a recluse. Sit down. Let's eat."

"I think I remember you," Dom offers, squinting at me as if placing me in a police lineup. "You graduated in Connor's class." Connor goes around the table to hug his younger brothers Weston and Maverick, but that's the extent of it.

"A year after him," I correct. Connor leads me closer to the table, where two empty chairs are wedged between Weston and Annette. They were expecting him to bring a girlfriend. Connor just failed to mention that it would be me. My fingers have turned to stone between Connor's, and I'm not sure he'll be able to escape my grip short of using a lever. The same kind one might use to break into a car.

I knew our parents had a beef, but I didn't think it would be this bad. As I grimace-smile at everyone around me, murmuring my greeting while melting into the wooden dining room chair, I try to perform a thought experiment. What if I showed up with Connor to my parents' house? Would they act like this? Would my father swear to the lord above in lieu of a greeting?

I don't get far in my scientific analysis, because Annette is slamming down dishes onto the table. I can't help but feel as if the angry breeze whooshing over the table is meant for me. Grayson tilts his head, jerking his chin toward Connor.

"Did you have a bunch of layovers or something?"

Connor lets out a terse sigh. "No, but the earlier flights were booked. We couldn't go until later."

"Hm." Grayson leans back in his chair, crossing his arms over his chest. Connor's grip on my hand tightens, and I get the feeling I've missed some sort of brotherly undertext.

"Don't worry, we flew business," Connor spits. Yes, there is definitely some brotherly undertext here.

"You live out west with Connor?" Dom leans forward, his authoritarian voice almost sounding as if it's coming from their father. Dom's neatly slicked walnut tresses distract me for a moment. He looks like a very stern Ken doll.

"Yes," I say, glancing around the table. This is an interrogation I wasn't entirely prepared for, because I'm not sure where the undercurrents are leading. Most of the brothers are looking at me, or between me and Connor. Only their parents are avoiding our gaze as if they're in that movie with Sandra Bullock and the blindfolds. Like if they look at me, they'll disintegrate into a weird zombie. "We actually work for the same company. That's how we...reconnected."

Not a lie, but it leaves plenty of room open for interpretation. Because that's what we're supposed to be doing here. Fooling his family into thinking we're not lifelong acquaintances who never exchanged words until last week.

"Oh, right," Dom says, a strange smile quirking his face. "What is it again? Some sort of national discount mailer...?"

Connor's gaze goes up to the ceiling, and I can feel his thigh go rock hard beneath our clasped hands. "It's E-bid. You remember, the nation's largest e-commerce marketplace?"

"Right." Dom adjusts his silverware for a moment, then snaps his gaze up to me. "Are you in the same department? Code monkeys or something?"

I look between Dom and Connor, not entirely sure what's going on here. Annette has bristled at my side, and I feel as if the nearby window is going to crack from pent-up pressure.

"Code poets, you mean," Connor corrects with a tight grin. "And no. She's in HR."

"I could never do what Connor does," I add quickly, sensing the need for someone to speak up for him. Clearly his brothers have some sort of holier-than-thou battle going on. Annette has started a serving bowl around the table—mixed greens. Ranch dressing sits on the table, which is the only option that matters. "They really test the developers at E-bid. The company has been expanding so much, and the challenges have been really..." My voice withers as Mr. Daly mutters something to Dom, and I get the sense it's about me. "Challenging."

Connor clears his throat and slings his arm over the back of my chair. My cheeks are hot, so it's probably time to shut up.

"When's the funeral?" Connor asks minutes later after the dining room has grown deafening with the sounds of scraping knives and sighs.

"Thursday." Annette has softened slightly, but instead of tension wringing at her features, it's tiredness. I would squeeze her hand, but I'm afraid she might karate chop me if I tried.

Connor nods, looking down at his plate. He's loaded it up with steak and potatoes and salad. I can barely taste my food since I'm so distracted by the hurricane brewing at the table. Wondering if we'll all get drenched in the aftermath, or if it'll just dissipate into a harmless cloud cover.

Weston pipes up. "How long will y'all be staying?"

Grayson snorts. "Y'all? Were in the north, pal."

"I was down south recently," Weston replies. "Cut me a break. It sticks."

"I'm here through the weekend, and a few more days," Dom says before shoving a forkful of potatoes into his mouth.

"We'll be here for the next two weeks. So you better get used to what it's like to have your older brother around again," Connor says, ruffling Weston's hair.

Maverick's dark gaze flits around the table. He looks gaunt, in the way that only hard-partying twenty-somethings can. "You're not staying in my room, are you?"

"Oh, that's right." Annette dabs at her mouth with her cloth napkin. "Connor, your old room is now Maverick's new room."

Connor scoffs good-naturedly. "But I wanted to show Kins all the things I scribbled on the inside of my closet."

*Kins.* I fight a cheesy grin. He has a nickname for me already. Even if it's born out of this ruse, it still feels good to hear it.

"I get the big room," Grayson pipes up. "I'm here for a month. I need the space."

"Oh, no," Maverick retorts. "The big room is mine."

"I'm older than you. I get it," Grayson continues.

"Well I live here, so I get dibs," he shoots back.

"Grayson actually has an income," Mr. Daly pipes up, "so I think he wins the big room."

"I *make money.*" Maverick's glare is trained on his dad. "Not like any of you would notice, since it's not six figures."

"Boys." Annette's warning tone is clear.

"Your allowance from Dad doesn't count," Dom cracks.

"You know what? Fuck you, Dom," Maverick spits. There's a flurry at the table while Dom acts affronted and Mr. Daly grumbles his opposition. I keep my head down, focusing intently on the slice of red onion in my salad. The outburst is sort of exciting, if only because I recognize it. All this roiling tension under the surface, all the intense stares and unspoken sentiments feel like home to me. Maybe the Dalys aren't so different after all.

"You don't have to get so *ruffled*." Even I can agree that Dom's condescension is rolling off in thick, sticky waves. I give him a 2/10 for hiding his true opinion. "I don't live here anymore. I actually left my hometown to further my education."

Annette slams her fork down. That's the warning shot. Grayson's eyes are narrowed, but I can't quite tell whose side he's on.

"Not everybody has to go straight to college after high school," Weston pipes up. I can tell he's the nicest Daly boy. He's got something about him that screams *peace and love*, and it's not just his longish hippie hair.

"Of course not. But most people take a gap *year*, not gap *decade*."

"Jesus Christ, Dom, you're worse than Dad," Maverick barks, and as Grayson opens his mouth to add something to the discussion, Annette's voice slices through the dining room.

"BOYS. ENOUGH."

The table falls silent. Maverick scowls at his plate, and Connor looks at me with the most pitiful sort of grimace. I can read it all over his face: *Welcome to my family.*

But it's okay. Because his fingers are still laced through mine, and for a moment, I can tap into something inside me that believes the way our eyes are locking might have a whiff of truth behind the intensity.

Like maybe he's feeling the same current running between our hands.

Like I might be able to have a man like Connor at my side someday.

# CHAPTER SIX

CONNOR

That dinner was *Guinness Book of World Records*-style horrible. It probably won several categories by default—Worst Pre-Funeral Family Reunion, Midwest Edition, followed by Most Awkward Dinner as Judged by Quantity and Frequency of Throats Cleared.

Really, in the grand scheme of things, bringing Kinsley here was genius in both the diabolical and unexpected sub-genres. Diabolically genius because I'd pissed my dad off even more than planned, which brought Mom right along with him; and unexpectedly genius because Kinsley's presence at my side was far more grounding and reassuring than I'd imagined possible.

I held Kinsley's hand at every point during the dinner that we weren't eating, a fact I didn't even realize until Mom was clearing plates and I finally figured out why my hand was sweating. It was hard not to hang on to her. Our hands fit well together, which isn't a thing I knew was possible before tonight. I've held hands with *plenty* of girls, and I'm not saying that as a metaphor for sex.

Kinsley stood up for me multiple times during that awkward and hellish journey through the Daly family dysfunction. Even though my parents acted as if she wasn't there the entire time. I probably need to up her compensation for agreeing to this. Even I couldn't have predicted this brutally frigid reception. I thought Dad would put on a forced friendly front and complain viciously to Mom behind closed doors, like any normal American.

Once dinner is over and my brothers have completed their jousting match over who gets which bedroom, I am feeling far superior, since I have been *the* most laidback about the bedroom thing. I grin my way up the staircase, Kinsley trailing behind me. We head for the last bedroom, which has a sunrise-facing window I've always particularly liked. I push open the door, and the cozy guest bedroom greets us.

In front of us, the plush queen-size bed is neatly made, the head of the white comforter pulled back. Beckoning us into its comfort.

Something is off, but I can't tell what.

Kinsley speaks. "I thought you said there were two twin beds?"

*Shit.* That's what it is. I roll our luggage into the bedroom and shut the door.

"There were." I frown. "In my old room."

She's gnawing at the inside of her lip, glancing between me and the bed.

"Will this be okay?" I ask, suddenly worried I've overstepped our tenuous boundaries. Clutching her hand in a vice grip for the duration of dinner? Fine. But sharing a bed, even platonically? This could be the deal breaker. "I can sleep on top of the covers, if you want, or bring a sleeping bag—"

"It'll be fine." She waves her hand dismissively and shrugs, heading for the bed. "I wouldn't want you to sleep on the floor on my account."

I smirk, unable to pass up the chance for a joke. "I didn't mean *I* would be sleeping on the floor."

She narrows her eyes, a laugh bursting out of her. "I can't imagine you'd drag me two thousand miles for that encounter with your parents *and* make me sleep on the floor."

My laughter turns into a sigh. "Sorry about that. I didn't think it would be that bad. Honestly."

She shrugs again, picking at something on the comforter. "I know our parents always had issues. I just didn't think it would make them act like that."

I ease onto the bed next to her, even though I could have sat anywhere else in the room: the other side of the bed, in the chair facing the bathroom, or hell, even on the gray Berber carpet. But being near Kinsley has already burrowed in like a habit. Even though no eyes are watching us. "Do you think your parents would act the same?"

A sigh bursts out of her. "I don't know. Maybe. It's weird to think that we're being the adults here."

Regret crashes through me. *Am* I being the adult here? My reasons for bringing Kinsley are hardly noble. Sure, I bought her plane ticket. But also, I needed her presence to get back at a small handful of people. And that seems like the opposite of mature.

"Listen. We're gonna have a great time," I say, channeling my hopes into words. "My parents will loosen up. But we won't even be here much. We can go do whatever we want. This is vacay, baby."

She sends me a curious glance. "Whatever we want, huh?"

I can't help it. My mind goes straight to sex. I'm 100 percent man and 50 percent beast. Which makes for some sort of mathematically impossible species. My gaze drops to her lips. God, she's got great lips. Maybe we can slightly expand the list of Bayshore-relationship activities.

"Absolutely." The side of my body closest to hers is getting hot from curiosity. She's not my type—not even a little. But I'm still wondering what it might be like to go there with her.

"You know I brought twenty books with me, right?" she says. And like that, the fire under my skin goes out. Not because books aren't sexy—trust me, they are—but because I realize she wasn't heading down the same kiss-curious path I was. She meant *books*. Because she is not a man beast who would already have her half undressed if she'd allow it.

"Like I said." I push to my feet. More distance is probably wise. Sitting that close to her is messing with my head. "We're creating this vacay. And if that includes starting your own book club, so be it."

She smiles up at me, and there is something so pure and innocent in her gaze that my breath catches. The sunlight filtering into the room catches on her hair, highlighting the strawberry undertones there. Between her glistening braid and her sweet smiles, I decide in that moment that she is the definition of a sunbeam.

A sunbeam with slightly-too-large ears.

"What are you staring at?"

I blink, ripping my gaze off her. I have no idea how to cover my ass. "I was thinking about something else."

"And what was that?"

"That pizza place down at the four corners. Mama G's. You remember it?"

She snorts. "Does something about my face remind you of pizza?"

"Not exactly."

"Because if it does, I'm going to have high school nightmares tonight, and I might thrash you in my sleep."

"I'm pretty sure I have an old football helmet in the house somewhere. I'll be sure to wear that when I go to bed." I pause, dragging my gaze back over to her. "Pizza face."

Kinsley snickers, and her amusement feels like an accomplishment. I already know that Kinsley is my humor and mental equal after one sad night at the bar and an entire day of travel together. She can lob a joke as far as I can. And I'm realizing that although we're just pretending here in Bayshore, I actually want to spend time with her.

"What do you feel like doing tonight?" I head to my bag and start unpacking the basics—cologne, body wash, shaver, swimsuit. "I was thinking we might head down for a drink later. I'm sure Dad has already gotten out the alcohol in an attempt to smooth things over."

"Yeah. That sounds nice. I could use a stiff drink."

"You don't need to go see your parents?"

"I'll see them tomorrow." She flips her braid over her shoulder and unzips her olive drab duffel bag. She pulls out five books before reaching the first layer of clothing. I sneak glances while I arrange my own things on the dresser.

She disappears into the bathroom after a while, and when she re-emerges, she's dressed down in khaki shorts and an off-the-shoulder frilly top. It's sorta cute. Still vaguely reminiscent of the nineties, but hey, that decade is making a comeback anyway.

"I'm ready for alcohol when you are," she says.

"Just don't get too drunk and try to make out with me," I warn her as I breeze past and into the bathroom. I only said it because it's the only thing I've been thinking about for the last thirty minutes.

"Don't worry," her muffled voice carries through the door. "I wouldn't dream of consummating our fake relationship like that."

Consummating. The word on her lips makes me think of sex, *again*, and my mind flashes to the tanned shoulder sticking out from her top.

What a sleazeball. Coercing a woman into a vacation with the promise of plane tickets, only to come on to her once she's trapped in my parent's house?

I might be a man beast, but I do have morals buried somewhere deep inside.

If I know what's good for me, I need to keep these thoughts buried way below the surface. Kinsley is a non-option. I've always seen myself with the confident model types. Head-turning princesses who can rock a bikini and make my older brothers jealous. It's every man's dream, right?

But after the train wreck that was dating Tamara—who was everything I purportedly wanted—I'm not too eager to start anything with anyone.

Which means that if I had a list?

Kinsley would be at the bottom of it.

# CHAPTER SEVEN

KINSLEY

Annette and Damon go to bed early that night, just after nine p.m., which leaves all of us under forty gathered around the firepit in their postage-stamp backyard. A tall wooden fence closes us in, and rose bushes line the perimeter. It's fragrant and calming—even more so now that the Daly heads of household and their frosty glances have disappeared.

"So. Kinsley and Connor." Grayson is a little toasted already.

I get the sense that he's a good-natured prick. I guess all of the Daly brothers are. Except for Dom, of course. He just seems like a prick.

"Yeah." Connor takes a swig of his beer. He's finishing his second, and I've been nursing an enormous glass of moscato. "You got it right."

Grayson snorts and rubs at his face. "Definitely didn't see this coming."

"Well, why would you?" Maverick asks, something snide hidden in his tone. "Not like you and Connor live anywhere near each other."

"Yeah, but we see each other," Grayson says, pointing drunkenly at his younger brother.

"Oh, do you?" Maverick goads. The flames licking out of the firepit make him look even more haunted than normal. His longish pitch-black hair is swept over his forehead. "Like you see us here at home?"

"Oh, come on," Grayson replies. "It's not like you've ever come out to see me."

"I don't need to visit New York again to know that I still hate it," Dom mutters.

Grayson's lips thin, but he just leans more forward, as if blocking Dom out of his line of sight. He's staring at Maverick across the fire pit. "Mav, come out and see me. Do it. I'll buy your ticket."

Maverick shrugs. "I might."

"I'll get you a job, too, if that's what you want. You could be making a hundred grand in a year."

Weston has been watching everyone converse, sunk back in his Adirondack chair. He's had a root beer in his hands for about an hour, and I'm not sure if he's taken a sip.

Dom heads into the house for a moment. When he comes out, he's holding a freshly refilled tumbler of what I am pretty sure is straight whiskey. Grayson peers at him with one eye pinched shut.

"Didn't bring one for me?"

"I wasn't aware you liked drinking quality beverages," Dom responds before easing back into his seat. Grayson has a Corona in his hand, which to me seems quality enough.

Grayson scoffs, and Connor clears his throat. He sends a glance my way before he opens his mouth to speak, which makes me sit up. In case I might be called upon for some fictitious piece of our couple's history.

"So, are either of you seeing anyone?" Connor has directed the question to Dom and Grayson. We already became privy to Maverick's lack of girlfriend earlier, when Grayson stole his phone and found current text conversations with *three* girls.

Grayson exhales loudly, leaning back into his chair. "Who has time? I'm too busy making money."

"Same. Except, making money *and* saving people's lives," Dom says.

"Oh, right," Grayson mutters. "Can't forget that. Dr. Dom."

"You guys are missing out." Connor's hand shoots out, grabbing mine. He squeezes it gently before charging ahead. "Love is the sweetest gift. I thought I had it all before Kinsley. And now..."

I offer a small smile to his brothers' disbelieving faces from across the fire pit. This sounds ridiculous. Or maybe it only sounds that way to me because I know what a crock of shit it is.

"Isn't that right, Kins?" Connor turns to me, his blue eyes glinting in the light of the fire. And then suddenly, I'm lost in his gaze, absolutely tumbling through space and time to meet him in his crystalline tractor beam.

"Oh. *God*." A weak laugh escapes me, and I finally rip my gaze off Connor. "I thought I knew what love was before I met this guy." I jerk my thumb toward Connor for emphasis, even though it's totally unnecessary. "I was wrong. He..." My gaze drifts back toward him, and my voice disappears for a moment. "He shook my world up. Like a snow globe."

There's warmth in his gaze as he watches me, and I can practically hear him saying *Yes, yes, that was great*, as I finish talking.

"You don't seem very affectionate," Dom remarks, sniffing.

"Says the least affectionate man in the world," Grayson adds.

Connor scoffs. "Trust me. We're affectionate. I told her we'd need to tone it down this weekend because of all the family." His arm shoots out around my shoulders, bringing me closer to him. We're in separate chairs, so this is an awkward move. "Aren't we so affectionate, babe?"

"Oh," I start, swallowing a knot of nervousness. But when I look up at Connor's face, the mischief in his gaze sparks something inside me. "The *most* affectionate. If we had an affection-o-meter..."

"To measure the output of our affection?" He prompts.

"Mm-hmm. Our reading would be off the charts. Like...3500 megahertz."

"That's really high," Connor says, a smile curling his lips.

"It's actually in the *dangerous* territory, according to recent studies." It's too easy to bullshit with him. And I love that this is flowing out of us.

"Ugh. You two *are* meant to be together," Dom scoffs.

Grayson twists to look at Dom. "You are the living definition of curmudgeon. Why can't you be happy for Connor? It's hard for the middle kid to find success. Especially in a family like ours."

Maverick snickers. "Jesus, Gray."

When Connor scoffs, Gray is quick to cover his trail. "I'm *kidding*. The middle kid thing—it's just a theory. It's half-baked. It doesn't even...it doesn't even matter." He's finished his beer and opened another. This behind-the-scenes peek at the Daly household is more fascinating than it is offensive. Of course I'm not the one getting rained on—Connor is.

But Grayson isn't totally wrong in what he said. The alcohol is making the truth flow more freely—what his version might be of it—and his comments make me piece together something very important about Connor and me.

We're both middle children, and the way his older brothers are treating him feels too familiar to be coincidence. My older sister treated me the same way, and my younger sister struck a balance between Weston and Maverick. So in a way, maybe Connor and I really *are* the same.

"We don't need them to judge our affection," Connor says, turning to me. But he's saying it loud enough that I know it's also meant for his brothers. He leans forward, tilting his forehead toward me, which prompts me to do the same.

"They wouldn't be good judges," I say. Our foreheads touch, and the grin that erupts on my face feels too silly to be forced. No, this is all real with Connor. Just my inner teenybopper *freaking out* that I'm touching Connor's forehead. Maybe I'll never wash it ever again. Maybe I'll circle it with permanent marker so I'll never forget.

"Horrible judges," Connor says, and then brushes his nose against mine. I bite my bottom lip reflexively, my thighs squeezing together. I catch whiffs of his scent despite the woody smoke around us. He's leather wrapped in spice, and my eyes flutter shut as I relish his masculine scent. "They don't even know about that time we broke the affection-o-meter."

Connor's hand finds mine again, and he laces his fingers through mine. I giggle—*honest to God giggling* like I used to absolutely rip my sister apart for when she was a senior in high school and acting a fool with her flavor of the week. This is what I get, though. The fullest dose of *I told you so*. I never felt like this with my ex, that's for damn sure.

"Okay, guys. You made your point," Grayson says, waving us off.

"No, no." Connor tugs my Adirondack closer so that the arm rests bump together. His hot palm finds my bare knee, and I swear to God my panties are soaked on the spot. "We're not done making it."

"You might want to make it up in your room," Maverick muses. "You can make your point all night long, even."

"Just don't wake up the rest of us," Weston cracks.

"Only Dom's at risk," Connor says, swinging his gaze toward his eldest brother. "You're right next door."

"Oh, Jesus." Dom shakes his head. "I didn't leave my penthouse this week only to rejoin a fraternity."

"You probably should have stayed in Cleveland, then," Grayson mutters.

"Don't worry. We'll wrap up beer pong by midnight," Connor says, swinging that electric blue gaze back my way, his shit-eating grin out in full force.

If I didn't know better, I'd say that the warmth in his eyes really was reserved for me.

As if maybe he saw me as someone he really could spend the night with—and then some.

I should know better than that. First of all, because this is pretend.

But more than that? Because I already learned what happens in relationships. I know what happens when you trust a handsome face and dimpled grins.

Not just heartbreak, but heart shatter. My ex wasn't half as hot as Connor, but that's only because most men aren't. He was fully handsome and 100 percent manipulative. He taught me the extent of my flaws. Just how deep and pervasive they are; how they meant that nobody else, and barely even he, could ever love me.

So I know the truth. Girls like me aren't meant for men like Connor. No matter how warm and convincing it might feel at their side.

Which means that I can't read into this. Into *any* of this.

And hell, I hope I can remember that while we're in Bayshore.

# CHAPTER EIGHT

KINSLEY

The first night under the Daly roof is more stressful than I imagined. Because once the lights flick off, it's just Connor and me in the queen bed. Barely clothed and *lying there*.

I measure my breaths for the longest time, trying to fake a steady rhythm while simultaneously listening to hear if he's fallen asleep. We are not touching at all—in fact, I've scooted to the farthest reaches of the bed, curled up on my side, in a position that becomes uncomfortable approximately twenty seconds in. But I can't move. Because we're supposed to be falling asleep.

My mind races for what feels like hours. I thought downing all that moscato would help me fall asleep, but Connor's weight on the other half of the bed erases any vestige of sleepiness. All I can think is, *Male body nearby!!!! MALE. BODY. NEAR. BY.* As if some sort of purity alarm is going off inside me.

Despite the elevated mental activity, I do somehow fall asleep. Because the next time I'm aware of anything, sunlight is streaming into the bedroom and I am *warm*.

The Dalys keep their house this side of frigid, but I've managed to make quite the nest in this bed. And man, it's comfortable. Pillow-top mattress and all. I yawn, and when I nestle back into my comfortable spot, I realize my cheek has stuck to something.

I don't open my eyes or even move much, because that's against first-morning-of-vacation rules. I need to sleep in and enjoy this for as long as I possibly can. I'll slowly use my awakening senses to figure out the mystery stick in my own time.

I tilt my head, and my temple presses into something warm. Hard, even. I draw a deep breath, shifting beneath the sheets. They're, like, 8,000 count or something and impossibly soft. My arm moves from its resting spot, and that's when I notice it wasn't resting on the bed.

I'm pretty sure I have my arm flung over Connor's torso.

This makes the purity alarm start screaming again, and I jolt up.

Connor's torso is beneath me. Not the neutral expanse of unoccupied bed as I had assumed.

No. His naked, perfectly toned and tan torso.

I blink, taking it in. And that unsightly spot on his chest?

Yeah, my dried drool.

My hand shoots to my face, and I can feel the crusty trail leading from my mouth. *Oh please God, no.* I bolt out of bed before he can wake up and *see* this. Or realize that I draped myself across him like a needy little nymph.

I stumble toward the bathroom attached to the bedroom. The early morning sunlight grates on my sensibilities, and I actually run into the doorframe before I make it inside. The door shuts much harder than I intend, and I wince inside. Bull in a china shop at eight a.m. over here.

I clean myself up as quickly as possible, brushing my teeth for good measure, and then snag my morning pee. I walk back into the bedroom, readier than ever to continue sleeping in.

Connor is sitting up in the bed, rubbing at his eyes. The sheets are gathered around his hips, and his belly creases as he leans forward slightly.

"Morning," he says, looking at me with one eye pinched shut.

The sight of him is too glorious to comprehend. He is pure tousled bedhead and bleary baby blues. Half of him looks ready to flop backwards and keep sleeping.

"Are you getting up?" I climb back into the bed and stick to my half of the bed. I settle in, but I know that sleep will elude me. Now that he's up, I want to be up, too.

"Yeah." He yawns, then pauses before saying, "I had a dream we were spooning."

I snort, but then I spot the dried drool on his chest and freeze. "You should take a shower."

"Do I stink?"

"No, it's just—" I have no good reason waiting in the wings for *why*. "I like to start my day with a shower. I thought you did too."

"I do, actually." He stretches and then finally rolls out of bed. And this is when I blessedly receive the answer to my question. He sleeps in boxer briefs.

Hallelujah, I've seen the flaccid outline of his cock.

He glances at me, and I jerk my gaze over to the suitcases. I must document this occasion in my journal. This is a major victory for sixteen-year-old me.

"Sorry," he says. "Is this weird? I'm used to sleeping in my underwear, so…"

I look down at my puritan night ensemble: long pants, long-sleeved cotton shirt, and the lemur cartoons printed across all of it. "No, no. It's fine. I would have slept in my underwear like I normally do too, but…" I gesture to my pajamas. "I just got these, so I need to wear them."

"They're cute," he says offhandedly, but what he probably means is, *You're weird.* "Did you sleep well?" He pauses at the dresser. His calves are sculpted. His ass is comprised of two small melons. Every part of him is perfect, and I can't help but stare.

I nod so hard, I almost give myself an issue for my chiropractor to sort out. "Yes. Yes. Oh, yes. It was great. Had a great time. I mean sleep."

He cracks a grin, which I spot through the mirror. "Good. I'm sure it's much better than the floor."

"Ha. *You* would be the one on the floor, not me." I roll back out of bed, heading for my suitcase. "Or is chivalry dead in Bayshore?"

He snorts. "The bar for chivalry has gone way down, if that's all it takes."

Heat zips through me, though I can't say why. Any sign from him I'm eager to translate into a profession of attraction, so it's not hard to warp his words into something more. But I remind myself I'm being silly. Ridiculous, even. We are work colleagues and, during our time in Bayshore, co-conspirators. That is *it.*

All I can think of in response is, *I'd like to see something on you go way up.* But that is not only wildly inappropriate, it is also the least sexy way to tell someone you'd like to bone. So no. Better to say nothing and maintain my last shred of mystery and cool instead of blow it to smithereens on day two.

Connor scoops up a new pair of boxers and some other sundries from the dresser and nods my way as he heads into the bathroom. "I'll be quick. Then we can head down for breakfast."

The bathroom door clicks shut, and I sink back onto the bed, gnawing on a nail. I should take this time to get dressed, but all I can think about is Connor. I'm totally dependent on him suddenly. Sure, I could waltz downstairs and grab breakfast and coffee on my own, but I won't risk that frigid reception waiting for me from his parents. I need Connor with me *at all times.*

And then, once it's acceptable to escape, I will run to my parent's house—sans Connor—and pretend this is one giant happy happenstance.

While the shower runs, I try to imagine what the next two weeks will really look like. Visits to the lake: obviously. More bonfires with the Daly brothers: most likely. Continued frostiness from the parents: very probable.

But what about visiting my family? Once I see my parents today, they'll want to claim *all* of my available evenings. Both of my sisters live elsewhere; my younger sister Katie just finished her junior year of college in Cincinnati, but she's living down there for a summer internship. My older sister Kestrel lives in Columbus, but she barely makes it home with her crazy schedule. So when I show up? Mom and Dad are gonna try to squeeze their time for all three of us out of me alone.

And since I've decided that I'm here strictly as a surprise family-and-friends tour, I will not be telling my parents that I'm staying with the Dalys, much less dating Connor in any respect. Because after yesterday, I realized the sad truth. My parents *would* probably give Connor a similar reception as Annette and Damon gave me.

Connor coughs from inside the bathroom, which sets me on high alert. God, he's in there right now, *completely naked.* I wonder if he uses a loofah. Or maybe a bar of soap and a washcloth. Gliding over his taut muscles, slick and slippery.

Shower sex. It's something I love but have only ever done once in my life. The early days with my ex were the best—the days when he acted like my biggest fan—and in those dreamy, sexy times we did a few things worth reminiscing about. But that period lasted about three weeks, and then it was a slow downhill trek to the bottom of an abandoned well.

Shower sex with Connor? The thought alone seems too scandalous to even consider. A chill races up my spine. My thoughts are hopelessly riveted on imagining the steamy, slippery scenes that I could create with him—*if only he were ever attracted to me*—while I slip out of my lemur pajamas. He seems like an attentive lover. Someone who would at least kiss me before shoving his hands down my pants, like the majority of my college hookups failed to do. I'm moving in a daze, caught halfway between reality and my fantasy shower world, when the bathroom door swings open.

I freeze. I'm wearing pink granny panties and a tank top. My cheeks flame instantly, and I grimace, hurrying to dress. I had so much time to get ready—if only I hadn't squandered it in the washcloth vs. loofa debate.

I bend down in front of my suitcase, pawing through the contents for my jean shorts. Dammit, I know I brought them. I toss aside *Pride and Prejudice,* grunting. My entire body is hot, and I can't tell if it's because Connor is greedily gobbling up the view (which I hope), or if my embarrassment is slowly incinerating me from the inside out (which I suspect).

I snag my jean shorts and hurry to slide them on, hopping from one foot to another. When I have them buttoned, I turn around, affecting my best *I'm used to being caught half-naked in front of heartthrobs* smile.

Connor is facing away from me at the dresser, which makes my smile droop a little. So he wasn't staring at me, gobbling up my half-naked glory. Why would he even care about my tomboy body? He dated Tamara after all, and she has the type of body that puts hourglasses to shame.

I head back to the bed to make my side, and the steam rolling out of the bathroom finally hits me. It is heat and musk and cologne all wrapped up into one tantalizing mist. Connor tugs on a muscle shirt to go with his gym shorts, allowing those tanned biceps to come out and play.

"Are you ready for breakfast?" He doesn't look at me as he asks it, grabbing his wallet off the dresser, followed by his phone.

"Of course. And then I think I'll head out after we eat and go spend the day with my parents."

"Sweet. I'll probably head to the beach for a while. Text me when you plan on coming back, and we can meet up."

He runs a hand through his damp, sandy-blond hair, exposing the darker hair of his armpit. My core tightens—yes, his armpit hair is erotic—and I grab for my enormous purse. He looks at me, something suspicious in his gaze. As if he's about to accuse me of something or tell me that I've got an enormous booger hanging out of my nose.

I meet his gaze for the briefest of seconds, then I glide toward the door. Whatever it is, I'm not ready to hear it. "You ready?"

He follows me, and whatever he was about to bring up fades into obscurity. "Yes, sweetie," he says, the smile more than evident in his voice.

I grin as I lead the way down the hallway, bringing us closer to this episode of Fake-Dating the Daly Brother, Episode #2.

And one can only imagine what this day will bring.

# CHAPTER NINE

CONNOR

Kinley doesn't text me to meet up at all that afternoon or evening. Which is fine. Because she's her own woman with her own life. And we're not dating.

Even though two days of pretending to date has me in boyfriend mode.

I spend the day as lazily and thoroughly as possible. Grayson and I head to the docks to ride out onto the lake on the two family Jet Skis. We crash through white caps and chase each other until we get hungry, then grab lunch at a diner downtown and spend a grand total of $10 for both of us to eat. That sort of price is unthinkable where we live, so we leave a $20 tip because we're used to paying that much.

In the evening, I run into some high school buddies, and we grab a beer at High 5's which sits right on Briggs Bay. I'm drinking a local lager and watching sailboats drift on the tranquil blue water while double checking roughly every half hour to see if Kinsley has texted.

It's not because I need her here or because I think she needs me. Really, I sort of want her here. It would work out perfectly if she texted now, and I could tell her to come to High 5's and we'd grab a drink and talk a little bit more about those lemur pajamas. And then, once the buzz kicked in, I could convince her that we needed to kiss, because Grayson would inevitably arrive and, well, this ruse must be consistently reinforced.

But she doesn't text. So I close out the bar tab and start a slow, touristy pace down the boardwalk. The evening is completely aflame in golden, crimson-tinged sunlight. Couples dot the benches overlooking the bay. Seeing the contented smiles and clasped hands inspires a strange cocktail of emotions inside me.

I should be thinking of Tamara, who was my actual girlfriend for six months. But instead, my mind goes to Kinsley. It's a little too easy to pretend with her—last night around the firepit proved it. Somehow, the quips and laughs just flow around her.

And after this morning, I realize there's way more to Kinsley than she lets on. Like when I ran into her half-dressed in the bedroom. I wasn't expecting those shapely thighs or wide hips hiding under her preteen pajamas. And when she bent over in those whisper-thin pink panties? I about went into beast mode.

I pause on the boardwalk, gripping the wooden railing. She's cute. I can admit that much. Cute *and* funny. Besides, I knew for a fact that we'd been cuddling in our sleep without realizing it when I smelled her shampoo all over my shoulder before my shower. It didn't feel half bad having her in my arms, even though I was basically too asleep to realize it.

But the truth is that I'm so hard-up for intimacy, I'm acting like this is even remotely mutual. I lured her here as a favor, and now I'm creeping on her half-naked body in the one safe space I promised her inside my parent's house. Maybe I should find a hookup while I'm in Bayshore and be done with it. Then I'd stop creeping on Kinsley like some sort of predator.

I toy with this new idea while I stroll the boardwalk. I haven't used a dating app in a long time, mostly because it's nearly impossible for me to use social apps without a critical engineering eye. Still, I could put my work aside for once and find a booty call, right?

My phone buzzes while I'm trying to rally. It's Kinsley. Relief zips through me.

*KINSLEY: Ok I'm done being a doting daughter for the day. Where are you?*

*CONNOR: Waiting for you on the Boardwalk by High 5's.*

*KINSLEY: Sea ewe soon.*

I grin and select a bench so I can watch the bay while she heads over here. Living in San Diego has its fair share of beaches and water gazing, but Lake Erie is different. Even though I can see water as far as vision will allow, the lake doesn't have the same churning, infinite aspect as the ocean. If I get lost in the water here, I could end up in Canada, but more likely that little party island in the lake, Put-In-Bay. If I get lost in the water in San Diego? I might end up in Hawaii or even Tahiti. But more probably, I'd end up a shark's dinner.

But this is the water I grew up with. This is the lake that feels like home. I get lost in the lapping of the waves against the narrow gravel embankment below the boardwalk. Seagulls approach, cawing wildly over something. Probably French fries. It's usually French fries with them.

"Connor?"

Kinsley's voice jolts me out of my reverie. I twist to look up at her, and her smiling face is framed by the brilliant hues of the pending sunset. Wisps of sun-bleached blonde hair float away from her face. She's gripping the metal railing of the bench beside me, and for a moment I'm not sure if we should kiss. She's standing there like that—I'm looking up at her, waiting for something to do with my lips.

"Found you," she teases, sliding onto the bench. She shoves her hands under her thighs, stretching her long legs out in front of us. Her white Converse low tops scuff against the wooden path as she bops her legs up and down.

"How did you manage it?" The gulls nearby have started a bonafide commotion. They are shrieking and circling something nearby.

She shrugs. "I followed the gulls. They led me straight to you."

A laugh bursts out of me. "They are my loyal subjects, after all. They answer only to me." I nudge her with my shoulder. "How was your day?"

She looks over at me, pinching an eye shut against the sun behind me. "Pretty good. Went to some antique shops. Ate an enormous lunch. Napped on the couch."

"Vacay goals."

"Exactly. What about you?"

"Oh, you know. Lake, beer, and old friends. Perfect day in Bayshore."

She rolls her head around in a slow circle, exposing the length of her neck. I can't help but admire her. In fact, with this sunlight and this view, we need to take a picture.

"Let's take a selfie," I say, pulling out my phone.

"Really?"

"Yeah." I stand and urge her to join me with our backs facing the lake. "Come on, this is the golden hour."

She hops to her feet and joins me. I wrap my arm around her shoulders and pull her into me. "Okay, smile big."

The seagulls ramp up their protests behind us. A few criss-cross the frame in the background. I snap a picture as Kinsley snickers.

"What the hell is going on with them?" she asks.

"Unsatisfactory working conditions." I change the angle and snap a second picture mid-laugh. She swipes a few strands of hair out of her face. "Or maybe it's a seagulls' lib thing. They're holding the Bayshore Tea Party."

"This is history in the making! Take another," she urges.

"Okay, but the gulls are displeased." One lets out a screeching caw, and we both dissolve into laughter.

"Sorry, what did you say?" she jokes. "I couldn't hear you over the rebellion."

I snap a few more pictures, the lake glittering behind us, the seagull uprising in full view. We review the pictures on the bench, and at the last picture, Kinsley grabs the phone, squinting at something. She pinches the touch screen to zoom in, and then a sharp "Ha!" erupts from her.

She shows me the phone. A gull is angrily eyeing the camera in the last picture we took. It is fully pissed.

"Holy shit!" She dissolves into laughter, clutching my knee. I laugh until tears prick my eyes, and we leave the photo zoomed in on the seagull face for far too long.

"This needs to be a meme," I finally wheeze.

"What are you freaks up to?" A new voice breaks into our cocoon of hilarity. It's Maverick, peering down at us with a longboard tipped up against his hip.

In lieu of a greeting, I show him the picture we took. He snickers, looking out at the gull melee, which has calmed only slightly.

"One of you is pissing them off," Mav warns.

"God, don't we have anything we can give them?" I touch my pockets, but I know full well there are no snacks on me. "A half-petrified French fry? One granola crumb?"

"Not even a soggy piece of newspaper around here?" Kinsley asks.

Something in her tone sets me off again, and I dissolve into laughter again. Maverick shakes his head. "You guys are so weird."

"Come on, Mav, go find them a snack!" I implore.

"I am *not* getting you a seagull snack," Maverick deadpans. "I'm on my way home. Dad grilled out. You two coming?"

"Yeah, yeah." I sniff, wiping away one of the tears that spilled. Kinsley looks like she's still biting back laughter, and I can't look at her or else it'll set me off. I just know it. "You ready, Kins?"

She nods, avoiding my gaze. But we don't last a full minute trailing behind Maverick before we're both collapsed in laughter again. And God, it feels good to *laugh*. Real belly laughs which leave tears trickling down my cheeks. I haven't laughed like this in too long, and it's all because of a seagull and something inexplicable about Kinsley that makes me ready to have a good time.

I can't remember the last time I felt like this around someone.

I just know it's been too damn long.

# CHAPTER TEN



The birds are the first things I notice. Robins and bluebirds are chirping and calling and making a general ruckus. It feels early, maybe a little too early, to be waking up. But the air is cool and fragrant, exactly the type of early June morning that feels transcendent somehow in its coziness.

I shift under the covers, consciousness making small steps through me. We left the windows open last night to fill the room with Bayshore air, and the scent of freshly clipped grass fills the room. Someone on the block must have been up early taking care of grass duties. My entire left side is warm, and that's when I feel the weight of somebody else. Like, half on top of me.

Kinsley.

Again.

I crack open an eye and see her nuzzled into me. This is only the second time this has ever occurred—the second time we've ever shared a bed—but it seems like we've been doing it for much longer.

I stifle a yawn, shifting a bit so she fits better. Because it's nice to have someone cuddle up to you. Even if the pretenses for cuddling are largely a lie.

She mumbles something, burrowing deeper into my side. She's drawn her brows together, as if sleepily protesting my movement. I grin as I watch her. Her silky blonde hair is tugged behind her in a loose braid.  She's got the lemur long-sleeve on again, but the sheets tangled at her waist allow glimpses of the cotton shorts she chose last night. The tips of her toes peek out from the sheet at the end of the bed. Cotton candy pink nails.

I'm wide awake now. I shift again, and Kinsley slings an arm out, launching it over my waist. I bite back a laugh. In her dreamworld, she really doesn't want me going anywhere. I wonder what she's dreaming about. Whether or not I'm part of her fantasy, or maybe a stand-in for somebody else.

The rhythmic rise and fall of her chest lulls my eyes shut, but every part of my body is alert and aware. I can feel the silky union of her thigh touching mine. The butterfly tickles of her fingertips as her hand brushes over my belly with each inhale and exhale.

Is it so wrong for me to get hard? I have a half-naked woman—well, at least a third-naked, since that lemur shirt really covers *a lot*—draped over me, and I'm not the noblest of men. Besides, I haven't been able to get that view of her ass from yesterday out of my mind. I pinch my eyes shut, trying not to think of it now. Because the warmth and scent of her won't help, least of all now when I'm trapped at her side and unable to do a damn thing about it.

"Mrrnnmmgh?"

I don't have any idea what she's saying in her sleep. "Mm-hmm," I respond.

She sighs and cinches her arm tighter around my waist. She fits like a perfect addition in my arms. Honestly, I hope we do this every damn morning of our vacation.

A few moments of silence drift by, and then she inhales sharply. She goes rigid and jerks backward, all the way over to her side of the bed.

"Oh my God," she says, covering her face with her hands. "Oh my God, I'm so sorry. I didn't realize...I thought..."

I prop my head up on my arm and roll onto my side. "No worries, Kins."

Her throat bobs, and she looks around blearily, as if still getting her bearings. She fists the sheets and then sighs.

"Good morning," I add.

"Yeah." She laughs, rubbing at her face. "Good morning."

"Sleep well?"

She nods, sniffing. She still hasn't swept those periwinkle eyes my way, and I'm officially hankering for a glimpse. She grabs the end of her braid and tugs the hair tie off. "I was in the middle of a really weird dream."

"What sort of dream?" She pushes the hair tie over her wrist and works at unbraiding the bottom wisps of hair.

"Just...weird," she says, hopping off the bed.

"Did the seagulls show up?"

Her shoulders shake with laughter, and she twists around to grin at me. "Surprisingly, no."

She wanders into the bathroom, and I lie back on the bed, staring at the ceiling. My cock is going soft under the sheets, blessedly, since I don't think we're that far into our fake relationship to be showcasing post-spoon morning wood. The sink snaps on and then off again. There's some rummaging around in the drawers. I yawn, reaching for my phone on the nightstand. Today is the funeral, and I know it's going to be sad. Mom has been crying since last night, and today is going to tear her apart even more.

I'm scrolling mindlessly through news notifications when the bathroom door opens again. I glance at Kinsley, and the breath evaporates from my throat.

She doesn't look my way, so she doesn't notice I'm staring. Her hair is down—like *all the way down*—and I realize this is my first time seeing it like that. My cock pricks to life again. Surprise, surprise.

Her hair falls over her shoulders in gorgeous blonde waves, crimped from spending the night in her braid. She tucks some behind her ear as she rummages through her suitcase propped open on the armchair. Her lemur top has been replaced by a skintight tank top, and all I can think while she's facing away from me is, *When did Kinsley become a hottie?*

When she turns around, her nipples are hard points beneath the gray tank. I clear my throat, sitting up in bed.

"Don't forget," I say, feigning unaffectedness. "Funeral is at noon. We'll probably leave right after breakfast."

She nods, not looking at me as she holds up a pair of black slacks. She cocks a hip, then tosses them aside.

I fist the front of my hair. I'm fully hard again. I need a cold shower, stat.

"I'm going to go rinse off," I say, adjusting my junk underneath the sheets before I roll out of bed. I hurry to the bathroom before she's even turned around, and once the door is shut behind me, I cover my face with my hands.

What the fuck is wrong with me?

I bite back a groan as I flip the shower on. I think the real question is, when did Kinsley become a hottie in hiding? It had to have happened right before my eyes. I was blissfully unaware that this golden surf girl was hiding under my nose. Lithe, lean, and sparkly-eyed. All

I can imagine is her pretty eyes looking up at me while she kneels in front of me...wrapping those pink, plump lips around this cock that is absolutely throbbing for her.

I burst into the cold stream of water, but I don't last ten seconds before I'm fisting myself. Eyes pinched shut, I can see a highlight reel of the best of what could be, if only things were different. Kinsley bending over the side of the bed while I cup that tan curve of her ass. Hiking up her long, lean thigh onto the comforter. Hearing her giggle while I sink into her so slowly that I'll feel her tight pussy clenching, demanding more of me.

My orgasm happens in record time. The water washes away the white trail I leave on the side of the shower stall, and I lather down my body for good measure. And as I towel off after my cum-and-rinse, I feel a sort of satisfaction. Triumph, even, like I've figured out the loophole.

I imagined fucking her. So that should get it out of my system. Right?

When I come back into the bedroom, I make sure to leave my towel tied around my waist. She's in a plain black dress, pushing basic pearl earrings into her ears. Her hair is already pulled back into a fishtail braid.

Her eyes find mine in the mirror before they snap down to my body. And no, it's not hard to imagine her getting sidetracked by this fine physique. But the quick one-two glance reminds me of something I've noticed a lot with her.

She barely meets my gaze. And if she does dare to? It's only for a brief moment.

"You look nice," I say, my gaze riveted on her slender wrists as she smooths down the front pleat of her skirt. A smile graces her lips for a moment, and pink rushes to her cheeks.

"You too," she says, then she slaps her forehead. "I mean...sorry. That just flew out."

"Mm-hmm." I can't keep the satisfied smirk from my face. I didn't even realize I'd laid a trap, but she fell right into it.

"Force of habit," she goes on. "Like when the lady at the theater tells you to enjoy the movie and you say 'you too.'" She shakes her head, sighing.

"Right. But you can admit that I look nice without clothes on. I won't be offended."

The most nervous giggle I've ever heard slides out of her. In lieu of a response, she simply buries herself in digging for something in her luggage.

That didn't go exactly as planned, which makes me wonder if I'm really being a creep. Liking your own appearance is one thing. Assuming everyone else does, too, and then being really wrong is on the other end of the Skeezy Spectrum.

I should stop with Kinsley. Even though her long blond hair makes my abs go hard and all the air in my body disappear for a touch too long.

"I'm gonna get changed," I warn her, and head to the dresser.

"I won't look," she promises.

This is not a tactic. At least, I don't think it is. But when I drop my towel, my skin prickles with anticipation. Wishing she *would* look. To see if even a bit of the tension thrumming under my skin might be alleviated, even temporarily.

Maybe I was wrong.

Maybe imagining sex with her once *didn't* get it out of my system.

I step into boxer briefs, and then the black dress pants that have been hanging in the closet since we arrived. I turn around as I'm buttoning them, and I catch her gaze for a scorching half second.

I could be wrong...but there was heat in that periwinkle glance.

Maybe she does like what she sees.

And if I know myself, I need to find out.

As soon as fucking possible.

# CHAPTER ELEVEN

KINSLEY

I cried a lot of tears for a woman I barely knew, for the mother of a lady who will barely look at me.

It's not hard, when the downtown Catholic church is absolutely brimming with family and community members, mourning the death of Ethel Pearson.

I'm sitting in the row behind the Daly brothers, which is reserved for significant others—I'm the only one—and then first cousins and more. Annette's brothers and sisters are further down her row. From what I can tell, I'm sitting next to cousin Matt who hails from the Cincinnati Pearsons. He looks equally as twenty-something and handsome as the entirety of the Daly brothers, which makes me wonder if it really is something in the gene pool that makes these guys *look like this.*

Connor is within an arm's reach, but I don't dare snag his attention during the mass. Once the funeral moves to the cemetery, Connor's hand doesn't leave mine. Everyone is teary-eyed, and Connor has massaged his forehead no fewer than a hundred times. When he's not holding my hand, he's hugging his mom. It's an all-around sad affair.

But the spell breaks slightly once we head to the Daly household for the post-funeral reception. Annette goes into host mode, and pictures of Ethel Pearson line the table. Family members are talking about her famous one-liners—"You can't lead a horse, make him drink, or damn near anything else"—while Annette laughs with her brother and sister about the most ridiculous of childhood memories.

It's weird being surrounded by so many Dalys, because A.) I am not one, and B.) my parents would probably shit themselves if they knew I had penetrated so deeply behind enemy lines. Honestly, I'm surprised Annette let me attend the funeral. I sort of expected a "Cabanas Stop Here" tape around the perimeter of the cemetery.

"Kinsley!" Connor's voice wafts in from the backyard. I step outside to join him, a slice of the bright mid-day sun breaking through the tree cover of their backyard. He's waiting for me with an outstretched arm, beckoning to me, and the smile on his face—directed only toward me—is so beguiling that I practically float toward him. When I approach, he snags his arm around my waist, bringing me solidly into his side. Leather and spice wash over me, and I about lose my footing and fall head over heels for this man.

But his voice snaps me out of my freefall.

"I was just talking to my cousins about us," he says jovially, and the subtle call to arms makes me snap my smile a little brighter.

"Oh, were you?" I send out my best winning grin. The one that says, *We're really a couple so no need to probe further, okay?*

"You two have a lovely life out west," the very prim-looking cousin says.

Dom and Grayson wander up, both holding beers. "What's going on over here?" Grayson says, clapping his stocky cousin on the back.

"We were hearing about Connor and Kinsley's wonderful life," Ms. Prim coos, smiling over at Connor. "It's so awesome that you work for E-bid."

Connor's grip around me cinches tighter as Dom's gaze swings over to us. "Oh, yes. Wonderful."

"I work for Emerson and Bennett," Grayson interjects, stepping forward. "Which is equal parts awesome and horrible."

The cousins struggle to place the city of origin of Grayson's firm, which prompts an overly long explanation of the various cities his firm operates in. While they're listening to Grayson, Connor lowers his lips to my ear.

"I think we should kiss."

The words sear through me like a surprise lightning bolt. Kiss? Kiss *Connor*? The very thing I've been fantasizing about doing since junior year of high school?

Abso-fucking-lutely.

"To prove what a special couple we are," he murmurs, and squeezes the top of my waist. To anybody else, it looks as if he's murmuring sweet nothings. I giggle, rolling my lips inward. I angle myself toward him more, finally daring to meet his gaze.

"Yeah?" I ask, nudging him with my shoulder.

From this angle, he's more gorgeous than ever. The corners of his eyes crinkle as he looks down at me. He wets his bottom lip, that leather and spice not only filling my senses but drowning me completely. I'm a goner. Send for the rescue boat. The S. S. Kinsley is headed to the bottom of Lake Erie.

His eyes search my face for a moment, and then he bridges the distance between our mouths, his lips landing against mine so softly, yet so *intensely*, that I have to silence a gasp. I grip the side of his arm, pushing up onto my tiptoes so that we can mash our lips together even more.

Because now that I've had a taste of him? I need all of him.

He smiles through the kiss, which leads to a second kiss, which leads to a very noticeable damp surge in my panties. My fingers dig into the sleeve of his white button-down.

"Jeez, guys," Grayson interjects a moment later, as we're rounding the corner into kiss number three. "Get a room."

Connor breaks away, and I collapse against him. My heart is pounding between my ears, and I'm not certain I'll be able to walk out of the backyard on my own two feet. Three kisses with Connor is all it takes to undo me. And we didn't even use our tongues.

"We do have a room, you know," he says to me, loud enough for the others to hear. I laugh weakly, because of course he's saying it for them. He doesn't mean it. Even though the fake kisses he gave me easily win first, second, and third place in the history of every kiss of my lifetime.

"Sorry, guys." I give his cousins an apologetic smile, but I'm not sorry at all. God, it's nice to play the coy girlfriend part. Connor doesn't move his arm from my waist, and he effortlessly rejoins the conversation about everybody's current work situation. I can barely focus on what they're saying. I couldn't care less, actually. I just want Connor to kiss me again.

But he doesn't, and the afternoon whiles on. Soon, Annette is bringing out the pasta salads, and Damon is firing up the grill. Some of the family members have left, but most of the cousins stay for dinner. The post-funeral remembrance slowly turns into a post-funeral party. Connor rolls his sleeves mid-way up his forearm, which nearly impregnates me on the spot. Once I see Annette has changed her clothes, I run to the bedroom to change into a thrifted sundress. It's strappy and long and full of cartoon suns, which seems perfect for this evening. Because, you know, *summer*.

When I come back down, Connor's gaze washes over me, leaving hot prickles in its wake. I can't tell if he likes what he sees or not.

"You should have told me you were going to change," he says once I rejoin him. "I would have come with you."

I gulp. Does he mean what I think he means? Nobody else is near us right now; the majority of the family is gathered around the patio tables, comparing the two types of pasta salads Annette made. While Grayson is loudly insisting the mayonnaise base is key, I realize that these words were meant just for me.

Finally.

"Well, the bedroom is still there," I offer, and as soon as the words come out, I realize I have no idea what I'm saying. I have no idea if he even meant what I thought he meant.

"Yeah."

*Yeah.* That's all he says, and then he looks over at his family, leaving me stewing in confusion. I read this *all* wrong. He probably simply wanted to change his clothes. Or maybe he would have suggested I put on something else. Maybe this dress is awful. It probably had nothing to do with continuing those kisses.

I finger the sides of my dress, wondering if I'd ever be bold enough to say the words, *Can we formally initiate a make-out session?* That might be the only way to clarify this. I could write it on a piece of paper, even, high-school style. Slip it to him when his brothers aren't looking. It would have two checkboxes, of course. *Do you want to formally initiate a make-out session with me upstairs? ABSOLUTELY NOT or HELL YES.*

Something has been left unsaid, but Weston calls him over suddenly. For some reason, Connor needs to weigh in on the subtleties of the pasta salad debate. I follow him, and Maverick has two big spoonfuls of each pasta salad while he passionately explains something about the acidity.

After Maverick's impassioned plea, Dom scoffs. "Whatever. You smoke a lot of pot, so you're always eating."

Maverick drops the spoons. Some pasta salad falls onto Grayson's pants, which makes him turn toward Dom angrily.

"Seriously?" he asks Dom.

"I didn't ruin your damn pants," Dom responds. "Mav dropped the spoon."

"Yeah, because you're *antagonizing him*," Grayson clarifies.

"Actually, all of you antagonize me," Maverick spits, getting to his feet.

"He's not wrong," Weston adds.

"Boys," Annette begins, even though she's halfway across the yard by the grill. Moms can sniff out a fight from up to five hundred yards away—I swear I read it in a science mag once.

The fray dissipates when Annette brings over a plate of hamburgers. There's a line of condiments carefully arranged, followed by napkins and paper plates with suns on them. I laugh and hold one up for Connor to see.

"Look. It matches my dress."

He smiles at me in a way that makes my core tighten. There's heat in his gaze, but more than that, I swear I catch a smidge of tenderness.

"You're such a sunbeam," he says, and the air goes tight between us across the table as we shuffle down the line toward the burgers. My hand is suspended mid-air, because the way he's looking at me has disabled my motor skills.

He's looking at me like he's gobbling me up. Like he doesn't just tolerate me, but that he actually likes me. Maybe even *wants* me.

Or maybe I'm so starved for affection that I'll see it anywhere.

At any rate, the lines are blurring. My panties are damp from wanting him, and I might not ever recover from our earlier kisses.

If this is what posing as Connor's girlfriend is going to be like for the next week and a half, I might not make it out of Bayshore alive.

# CHAPTER TWELVE

CONNOR

I don't sleep much that night. Whenever I drift off, I'm jerked back to consciousness by any sound or sigh from Kinsley. Every inch of my body is buzzing from wanting her, and I swear to God, I don't sleep more than three hours simply because my mind is in overdrive.

In the hours that I'm drifting between consciousness and restfulness, I come up with a new nickname for her. Sunny-kins. Because she is Sunny Kinsley. My sunbeam. Well, not *mine*. She's *a* sunbeam, who happens to be on loan to me while we're convincing my family she's mine. I sigh, turning away from her in the bed.

Dawn creeps into the margins of the windows. I can see the cobalt fringe to the pitch-black sky. It's got to be close to six, which means I've been replaying our kisses in my head for damn near twelve hours.

I want to continue those kisses so bad, I could karate chop a two-by-four and it would actually break, with zero martial arts training. *That's* how badly I want to push the envelope with her. I want to take it all the way. Big ears be damned.

I flop onto my back, forcing my eyes closed. I'm going to at least nap, so help me God. Now that the funeral is out of the way, the real vacation begins.

The only thing on my agenda is to put myself into painful proximity with Kinsley Cabana while beating back the urge to pull her slight frame on top of me and discover on a scale from one to velvet how sweet she is on the inside.

I adjust the pillow under my head while my cock throbs to life again. Thinking about velvet did *not* help things.

"Mrrgmmm." Kinsley's sleep protests are back, and she slings an arm over me. I grin from ear-to-ear up at the ceiling. This is what I get, I suppose. Platonic touches from a sleeping Sunny-kins.

I listen to her breathing. She shifts, which brings her hand dangerously close to my cock. I'm wearing underwear, so it's not like she's going to give me an accidental hand job. The rise and fall of my chest brings her hand nearer to and then farther away from my junk. My skin prickles across my shoulder blades.

I shift slightly, putting more space between her hand and my cock, which has gone half-hard. She mumbles something in her sleep that sounds suspiciously like "pasta." I stifle a laugh. I need to ask her later if she was dreaming about the pasta salad fight from yesterday.

She moves suddenly, burrowing into my side, her lips brushing against the curve of my neck. She wraps an arm around my ribcage, and one leg goes over top of my groin. Now my cock is trapped between her silky, warm thigh and my low belly.

And I am most definitely completely hard.

But hell if I'll move now. It feels too damn good to have her draped across me. I sigh, letting my eyes drift shut. Is this torture, or is this heaven? Something about Kinsley feels so soft and welcoming, as if I'm slipping on an old sweater I've had for years but completely forgot about. It doesn't make sense. We're basically strangers. Except there is something so familiar about her, I could swear we've been doing this for months instead of days.

I move so that I can sling my arm above her, removing it from its trapped position between us. She nuzzles closer, and I slip my arm beneath her head. I listen to her rhythmic breaths, hoping for sleep, but really my mind is on the fact that her breast is mashed against my chest. I would give anything to peel this pajama top off her, inch by lemur inch.

A car drives by outside. A little while later, I hear a lone seagull. And that's when I notice her breathing has quieted. My breaths whisper through the silent room. Her fingernails scrape into my skin below my rib cage.

I shift slightly, and Kinsley's leg flexes against me. Blood rushes to my cock all over again, like maybe *now* is the time I'll start paying attention to it. I swear I feel her hips jerk toward me, like maybe she's dreaming of me fucking her. Like maybe she wants this even half as badly as I do.

My senses go on high alert, trying to determine if she's awake and as conscious of our proximity as I am. I imagine the feathery brush of eyelashes against my side. Maybe she's come to and is wondering if *I'm* awake. Maybe her pussy is already wet from thinking about where else our kisses could lead.

I shift again, turning more onto my side, and she folds into me. My chin rests on the top of her head. Her hips thrust again, the inside of her thigh pushing up against my cock. Heat floods me all over again and there is *one* thing on my mind.

That had to be intentional.

I vote Kinsley is awake.

A gruff grunt escapes me, and I push my hips into her leg. She nuzzles into the hollow of my neck, her breath hitting behind my ear.

It's decided. This is torture.

And I've got only a couple more minutes before I need to go jack off in the shower.

"Kins." My voice is gruff so early in the morning. "Are you awake?"

She doesn't say anything at first, but she presses herself against me. When she speaks, her voice sounds a mile away. "Maybe."

I smile into the strawberry blonde flyaways at the top of her head. "Yeah?"

For a long moment, we're just breathing together, our chests rising and falling while the seconds melt away inside this steamy yet somehow innocent embrace.

"No," she finally says.

"Mmm." Blood is pumping through my veins so hard, so eager, that it laces my insanity with courage. I turn toward her, all the way now, and my palm finds the side of her thigh underneath the sheet.

So she doesn't mistake my intention. So she knows exactly where I want this reverie to go.

"Maybe we should keep dreaming, then," I murmur, digging my fingertips into her leg. She's heat and silk, and that's just at the part above her knee. She draws a deep breath, burrowing into the pillow. Her dark lashes flutter briefly, but she keeps her eyes closed.

"Mm-hmm."

I push my palm higher, starting a slow trek up her leg. She murmurs something, bucking her hips closer to me. My fingertips reach the hem of her cotton shorts, and I push up beneath the fabric, finding the goose-pimpled flesh beneath her ass cheek.

"Should I keep going?" My fingertips drift back and forth under the apple swell of her butt. She draws her brows together and nods furiously.

I wet my bottom lip, skipping my hand up over the fabric of her shorts until I find the waistband. I grip her and tug her closer, so that our bodies meet head on. If she hasn't felt my cock before, she does now.

I guide her leg up and over mine, so that she's half-straddling me. My groin presses into the sweet heat covered by her cotton shorts. She inhales shakily, eyes pinched shut.

I brush my cheek against hers, then allow my lips to graze her chin. I need another kiss. Immediately.

She giggles. "You're scruffy."

"You are." I brush my lips over top of hers, but she doesn't give it up to me.

She rolls her lips inward, ducking her head. "I have morning breath."

I flex my hips, and the steel ridge of my cock crashes into her pelvis. I trail my lips up along her jawline, until my breath hits her ear. "And?"

She shivers, hips bucking again. She wants it. Oh damn, she wants it. "It's not sexy."

"Morning breath is the last thing I care about." I slip my hands into her shorts, cupping the perfect apples of her ass cheeks. My cock is throbbing now. "Besides. We're dreaming, right?"

She grins, and this time, when I bring my lips to hers, she doesn't resist. In fact, she leads the way. Her mouth opens against mine, and our tongues crash together, urgent and hungry. The force there tells me how hungry she is for this. But she's not as hungry as I am.

I flip onto my back, bringing her with me. She straddles me from above, palms pressed to the mattress on either side of my head. One kiss bleeds into another, each one more drugging than the last. I'm tugging down the waistband of her shorts before I can think better of it, because I need to get in there.

When we finally break apart, her lips are pink and kiss bitten. Her hair is wild around her face, and I've never seen a more ecstatic sight. She blinks lazily, question marks in her periwinkle eyes.

"Take this off." I lift the hem of her lemur shirt. She watches me for a moment, then scrambles to comply. She lifts it up but gets stuck in the long sleeves somehow. She twists, grunting, dark blonde brows knit together in frustration.

"I can't—"

I laugh, tugging at a sleeve. She twists away from me, and her arm clears the hole. I push the shirt up and over her head, my gaze falling to her breasts as they meet the air. Her rosy pink nipples pebble under my gaze, and I cup them immediately. They are perky little handfuls that make my cock jump for the hundredth time. I swipe my thumbs over each nipple in turn while she watches my hands with a rounded mouth.

Finally, her head lolls back, and the moan rips out of her.

I found her sweet spot.

"Mmm." I buck underneath her again because I'm so horny for her I could die, but I'm not going to rush this. I dip my lips to meet a nipple, swiping my tongue over the tight point. Her thighs clench around my hips and she arches toward me, inviting more.

I cup her narrow ribcage in my palms, scraping my teeth over her nipple. She whimpers, her eyes drifting shut. She bucks again, her belly going tense. I can tell she is loving this, and watching her drift into outer space right before my eyes is more fascinating than I expected.

I wet my bottom lip as I switch from her left breast to the right one, humming low as I do so. Honestly, I could spend an hour here, laving attention over her perfect tits. I squeeze her ass cheeks, jerking her forward on top of my cock. She gasps, her palms finding the flat expanse of my chest.

Her eyes pop open, and her gaze finds mine, guilt written there.

She jerks once, and then twice, before a long, shuddery moan escapes her.

"Ohh, my God," she finally says, and then clamps a hand over her mouth.

I watch with wide eyes, unsure what just happened. "What, Kins?"

Her throat bobs, and then she shakes her head.

My chest is heaving as I assess her naked torso, then the pink cotton shorts hiding the part I am most desperate to know. I run my hand up the seam of her thighs, and she shivers visibly.

"I—"

It dawns on me. Her flushed cheeks. The sudden stop.

A grin overtakes my face.

I am the cockiest, happiest man in the world. "You came already, didn't you?"

# CHAPTER THIRTEEN

KINSLEY

Coming early was not included in the Fantasy Fuckfest timeline.

No, I had plans of proving my womanhood to him. To showing him how long and hard and then slow I would need it.

But the man insisted on licking my nipples like some sort of hyper-attentive sex god. Of course, he doesn't know that's my weak spot. Except he does now. Still, achieving orgasm in something like thirty seconds is embarrassing. He probably thinks I'm a virgin. Maybe I *am* a virgin and don't know it.

"You were just...the biting..."

His shit-eating grin is equal parts sexy and cocky, and the way his gaze washes over my naked torso makes me want to never move, not in a million years. I will live perched on top of Connor in this bedroom in Bayshore until my bones turn to dust.

The front of his hair is mussed and slightly wavy, lending his early morning look a touch of boyishness, but the intensity in his blue eyes betrays how much of a man he is. His big hands push over the dip in my waist. He's touched every inch of my exposed skin, his hands roaming like topography tools scanning my terrain.

And God, I never want him to stop.

"You should make a map," I blurt, and then I realize how little sense that makes.

"Of what? Your body?"

My cheeks flush, but not from embarrassment. "Yeah."

He dips his head down to my breasts again, taking each nipple in turn. I moan, my head tipping back.

"It's hard not to touch every inch of you," he says, which nearly makes me come again on the spot. "I'll be able to draw a map of your body from memory by the time I'm done with you."

Connor grips me by the hips and jerks me forward at the same time he thrusts upward, making his point long and stiff right between my legs. I whimper, my nipples straining at attention. I want his lips back on them. I arch my back, and his hooded gaze finds mine.

"Mmm." He takes one nipple between his plump lips and flicks his tongue back and forth over the tip. He's already serviced my weak spot more in ten minutes than my ex did in a full year. Another wave of pleasure shudders through me, and I cry out, digging my fingernails into the tanned ridge of his shoulder.

His skin rubs hot and electric and against mine. His big arms encircle my waist, bringing our bodies flush together. The sight of my breasts mashed against his perfect chest might haunt me for the rest of my life. I wish I could take a picture, but I don't want to interrupt the moment. And also, that might be weird. I shouldn't be a tourist in my own hot sex.

*Because I'm about to do it with Connor Daly.*

"I want to take these off," Connor whispers into my ear, his voice pure grit and sex. He's tugging at the waistband of my shorts. Another orgasm threatens at the edge of my composure, but I talk it down. Not now. I should at least wait for penetration this time.

But Connor slides his fingers beneath my shorts, up along my inner thigh, until his thumb is grazing the damp crotch of my panties. I whimper again, desire sliding hot and sticky through my limbs.

"Can I?" He nuzzles my neck, urging a response. His fingers press up along the edge of my panties, grazing my swollen lips. I tense, all the words inside me freezing in my throat.

A breath slides out of me while his fingers start a slow, teasing dance around my clit. He doesn't touch me, just grazes his fingertips in a torturous circle. The tension is as divine as it is intolerable. My muscles are steel while he takes his sweet time not touching me where I need it most.

"Come on," I urge finally, rocking my hips.

Connor slips his fingers beneath my panties, his thumb and forefinger finding the stiff peak of my clit. He rolls it, softly, slowly, until my entire body tightens and my second orgasm rockets through me.

My thighs clamp around him, and when the storm clears, I realize I've left crescent moon indents in his biceps.

"Number two," he says simply, and then coaxes a kiss out of me. "This is almost too easy."

I laugh weakly. Yeah. If it was so easy for him, why was it never like this with anyone else? Maybe it's the Heartthrob Quotient. The fact that my loins have been quivering for this man for years on end.

While I'm pondering this, Connor flips me back down onto the bed. I giggle, my arms going around his neck. My limbs are already lazy Jell-O, and we haven't even gotten to the good stuff. Although *all* of this is good. No, it's great. It's the fucking *best*.

Connor reaches for something on the nightstand, exposing rippling muscles down his side. He opens the drawer and fishes something out. His abs tighten as he comes back to the bed, and it's then that I finally realize what's about to happen.

He has a condom wrapper in his hand.

"Did you bring that?" I ask, my voice sounding small and distant.

"I asked Mav for one," Connor admits with a dimpled grin. He steps onto the floor for a moment, pushing his boxer briefs down. His eyes are on mine as his cock springs free from his underwear. A shiver rushes down my spine, and I get the sensation that he's gobbling this up, my naked reaction to his own nakedness.

My mouth rounds. His cock is rigid, straight and framed by tightly trimmed, dark hair. Now I see why people use the eggplant emoji. That vegetable might be the closest comparison, if one was forced to stay within the food pyramid. It curves ever so slightly upward, and as he climbs back onto the bed, his cock bobbing like the poster child for a virile twenty-something, excitement shudders through me.

*Connor Daly is about to fuck me.*

He makes quick work of my pajama shorts, pulling them down with restrained urgency. He tosses them across the room, then assesses my purple granny panties with a smile. He fists himself as he looks at me, which makes me squirm. I instinctively cover my boobs with my hands. I don't know why. He's probably looking things over and second guessing his choice.

"Everything up to snuff?" I ask, while dying internally at my choice of words. What am I even saying?

"Yeah." He wets his bottom lip, his gaze stuck on my lower belly. Then he reaches for my hands and puts them back at my sides. His lips find the point where my hip bone juts out, smoothing kisses above the panty line. His kisses stall once he kisses my mons through the cotton. His heated blue gaze finds mine.

"Just wondering if I should go for number three with my lips or my cock."

I pinch my eyes shut, groaning. "That is so fucking hot."

"What is?"

"What you just said." I throw my arm over my face, wriggling my hips. Because I can't watch. The tension of waiting—to come again, to be filled by him, to have his heat covering me once more—is too delicious to bear. I *need him.* "You pick."

He tugs my panties down a moment later, and I move in time to see his head disappear between my legs. He pushes my thighs wide open, veins bulging at the tops of his hands. His tongue finds me, crushed velvet against my swollen clit. I cry out but try to bite back the scream that wants to escape. My ass goes rock hard as he slurps and suckles at me, all his attention going to the one place that I never dreamed his lips would venture.

And lord, it doesn't take long. His tongue prods me, and then he flattens it over my clit. Back and forth, oh-so-slowly until the heat inside me becomes pressurized and I explode. My thighs quake as the third orgasm rips through me, hotter and faster than the last ones.

"Mmm." He nuzzles my clit with his nose, then passes his tongue over my dripping womanhood. I cannot believe he did that—willingly tasted my *juices*—but I'm too shaky to speak. While I'm a helpless mess on the bed, he slips a finger inside me, which prompts a moan from both of us. Like he's enjoying this even half as much as I am.

Which is impossible, because he hasn't gotten off yet.

"You are," he says, "so delicious."

He says this with two fingers buried inside me. I rock against him, urging something. Anything. He presses a kiss against my pulsing clit, and then he sits back. His cock has grown somehow, like before it was just hard, and now it's *petrified.*

I definitely shouldn't say that out loud.

If there's anything less sexy than comparing a man's glorious cock to something petrified, I don't want to hear it.

"Come here, sexy," he murmurs as he adjusts his position on the bed. He can't be talking about *me.* But I let him pull me up, and he urges me onto his lap. I collapse on top of him, his cock pressed against my folds. The naked steel of him against my most intimate area, with nothing between us, is a type of closeness I hadn't counted on this morning. But lord, this feels nice. Not just because we're in a carnal act designed to provide pleasure. It feels nice because I missed this type of closeness. Even though my ex was toxic, he showed me what it was like to share your most intimate parts with someone.

I haven't done this sort of thing with many men. But with Connor, it feels right. Heat pours off him as he rolls the condom onto his dick. I watch quietly—reverently, almost—as he does, and then he looks up at me, reaching for my braid. He tugs the hair tie off and makes quick work of my braid, until it's all undone and flowing over my shoulders. A smile tugs at his lips.

"I'll go slow," he says, bringing his mouth to mine, and then he kisses me like he means it. He grips my hips, and together we guide me into the right spot. His cockhead is bulging, and once it pops into me I gasp. But oh, the sensation is magical. Like trumpets are playing in the distance and my veins have lava pumping through them instead of blood. Every inch of my body lights up, electric and aware, as he pushes himself deeper inside of me. Stretching me to my limit.

I sink down, down, onto his glorious shaft. Our foreheads meet, and his breathing is labored while my pussy consumes him. He cups one of my breasts, as if making sure it hasn't gone anywhere. Once he's buried inside of me, every last inch of him, I moan into his chin.

"Connor," I say, almost like I'm begging.

"Fuck, I know," he responds. He sucks at his teeth, helping rock me in a slow circle on top of him. His cock fills me in a way I've never been filled before. "You feel so fucking good, Kins."

He grunts, flexing his hips once I start to move against him. I feel maxed out already, as if I've already come a hundred times. But we're just getting started. He wraps his arms around my waist, mashing my breasts against his chest again. He breathes into the hollow of my collar bone. Rocking upward into me while I do slow, lazy circles on top of him.

It feels too good. Like *way* too good. I can't even keep my eyes open, and I'm a breath away from coming. But dammit, I want to last. I want us to come *together*, so I can have this perfect first and last time with him.

Connor squeezes my sides, and then he slides his hands over my ass cheeks, spreading them. God, it feels so good to be manhandled by him. To have his hands everywhere on me for one glorious, dreamy morning. He jiggles my ass as he rocks up into me again, and then he groans.

"Fuuuuck, Kinsley."

My nipples graze his chest, and the slight friction there pushes me even closer to the edge I've been hanging onto by a thread. My core tightens, and I rock against him again, his cock buried so deep, I can't even speak.

"I'm close," he says, and I nod because I know. Because I've been close for *years* when it comes to this guy.

"I want to come with you," I whisper into his ear, and he sinks his teeth into my neck then, not like a vampire but like an impassioned lover. The unexpected move is a hard shove to my orgasm, and heat rockets through me, sticky and wild and free. I can't even see as the orgasm assaults me. Connor's arms go tight around my waist. He is coming too, moaning into my shoulder as his hips jerk, and we buck and writhe without rhythm.

My insides are goo, and once the pleasure recedes into a dull roar, I turn into useless putty in his arms. Connor laughs weakly, burying his lips into my hair.

Nobody says anything for a long time.

And before I know it, with Connor still buried inside me, I fall asleep in his arms.

# CHAPTER FOURTEEN

CONNOR

I awake with a start, so disoriented that I nearly fall out of bed. I'm naked, and my thighs hurt, and what the hell time is it?

I grope for my phone. It's almost two p.m. I rub at my eyes, the room full of sultry afternoon air. Shit. We left the windows open last night, and now it's humid. I roll out of bed and stumble toward the window, more bodily sensations revealing themselves. I'm sticky, like I forgot to take a shower last night. But oddly sated. Like maybe the sex-a-thon I dreamt with Kinsley could have happened.

My foot connects with something weird. I look down with one eye pinched shut.

A condom wrapper.

I pause mid-stride.

Holy hell, so that amazing sex with Kinsley *wasn't* a dream. And I actually haven't showered since that textbook demonstration of amazing sex.

I push the window down, and then I assess the room, rubbing at my face again. Consciousness makes tentative steps through me, bringing back the memories.

Long, sleepless night.

Volcanic sex with Kinsley in the morning.

And then a catatonic sleep afterward.

I check the bathroom, hoping she's in there. But she's not. I yawn, scratching at my chest before meandering back toward the bed. Well, that was a great start to the post-funeral vacation. More moments return to me as I head for a quick, cool shower. The slippery velvet of her pussy when I pushed my fingers inside her. That look on her face, half twisted between ecstasy and shock, when I eased my cock into her for the first time. And the way that blonde hair of hers tumbled over her shoulders. Fuck. This morning was epic, and I can't wait to recreate it.

When I finally find my phone, a text is waiting for me.

*KINSLEY: I'm spending the day with my parents. I'll text you when I'm ready to come back.*

I frown. That's sort of a bummer. Not that she doesn't have every right to spend the day with her parents, but what about more sex? I dress slowly, feeling significantly less tense than I have in probably six months. Sex with Kinsley wasn't just good, it was fucking fantastic. Shout it from the rooftops–style fantastic.

I've got on a perma-grin when I go downstairs. Mom spots me when she comes into the kitchen and tuts.

"You're up late today."

"I'm allowed to sleep in—I'm on vacation. Where is everyone?"

"Your father is at work. And your brothers went to the lake together."

"Aww. Everyone's bonding."

"I hope so." Mom sends me a look. "And you should join them."

I heave a sigh. It's no secret our family is fractured, to say the least. I don't want to be one of those millennials who blames Dad, but let's be real. Our dad is a competitive asshole who formed us in his image. So yeah, I called myself a competitive asshole by default.

But how could we avoid it? I change into my swim trunks and head down to the lake, a towel over my shoulder. I'm not sure who I'll find or what will be going on, but it doesn't matter. As long as I'm in the sun and water, that's all I need.

My flip-flops scuff down the sidewalk. The sun beats down on me, warming the tops of my shoulders as I walk past cute cottages and well-maintained two-story homes with wooden signs in the yard that declare their love for lake life. In our neighborhood, it's typical for people to name their homes, which means I've walked past The Shleigel Shanty, Buck Paradise, and Grover Groove on one block alone.

The perma-grin widens once my feet hit the sand at the end of the block. The beach is busy today, but I spot Grayson and the others a little down the shore. They're all playing beach volleyball, which obviously means I'm going to join. After all, competitive asshole here. I jog toward them, losing my sandal no fewer than three times in the process. I drop my stuff near theirs at the net pole.

Grayson shouts for me to get my ass in the game. Dom asks me if I even dare try. I decide to join Weston and Maverick's team, because they'll need the most help against our two assholier older brothers.

I join the game effortlessly, the cerulean sky streaked with wispy clouds as we volley back and forth. We're all shouting and laughing, and for once, we've struck that balance between competition and enjoying ourselves.

But of course, it doesn't last long. Maverick dives to return the ball, but he misses, which causes Dom to start laughing. Maverick insists the ball was out of bounds anyway, and then the fight over the unclear boundaries begins. Weston and I hang back as Mav argues his point against Dom and Gray.

"Where's your girlfriend?" Weston sniffs, shielding his eyes against the sunlight.

"With her parents." I wipe at my sweaty upper lip with the collar of my shirt. "Where's yours?"

Weston laughs. "I don't have one."

"Yeah, I know, I was being a dick." I squeeze my brother's shoulder. He's always been the pacifist in the family, opting out of the fights and competition as much as he could. But he's as much of an asshole as the rest of us. He just hides it better. "I should have asked, where's your boyfriend?"

Weston gives me the famous Daly side eye. "Wherever yours is."

I laugh. My brother likes women as much as the rest of the Daly men. That is to say: exclusively. But it's hard to not razz him. He *is* my little brother, after all.

Maverick comes over a moment later, sweating and scowling. "I'm done."

"Oh, come on, what happened?" I gesture toward Dom and Gray. "Don't let those two assholes ruin our fun."

"I'm not as asshole, I'm a gray-hole," Gray cracks.

"Con-hole here," I add.

"Dom-hole," Dom said, coming up with his hands on his hips.

"West-hole?" Weston asks.

Maverick smiles, and then finally, a laugh rips out of him. I glance around at my brothers, and they're all smiling too.

So this is what it feels like for us to get along for once. I wish Mom were here to see it.

"Listen, let's go fuck around on the Jet Skis," I suggest. Less competition and more open water is our best shot at maintaining the brotherly love. I get a round of agreement, and we head east down the beach, past striped beach towels and tanning teens.

While we walk, Mav occasionally stops to pick up rocks and skip them into the bay. Grayson falls into step beside me.

"Where's Ms. Ca-ba-na?" he asks, over-pronouncing her last name.

"Seeing her parents."

"Ah. Why aren't you there with her?"

"Because she's allowed to do her own thing, man." I shove Grayson a little. His questions are innocent enough, but I get the sense that he's testing me. Maybe I'm being paranoid.

We walk along for a little bit, our footsteps leaving weaving trails through the damp sand.

"I thought you were with that hot brunette," Grayson goes on, shoving his hands into his pockets. My chest tightens at the mention of her, but not because I miss her. Between hanging out with Kinsley and all the family time, I've barely thought of her. And even less after this morning.

Tamara and I never had the sort of explosive connection that Kinsley and I discovered today. We just looked good together and had the occasional nice night out. It was mostly fighting and frustration, though, interspersed with occasional make-up sex that promised better things on the horizon.

"Nah," I say, squinting into the horizon. Better to leave it at that.

Grayson rubs his chin for a moment, glancing at me like he knows a secret. "I'm surprised, I guess."

"About what?"

"She doesn't seem your type."

Irritation flashes through me. "And how would you know? You don't even know her." I pause. "You barely know *me*."

Grayson is quiet after that. He looks out toward the water. Conversation over, apparently. But his words stick with me. They grate at me on the surface, but as with all things my older brothers say, even their offhanded comments have barbs. They get beneath the skin.

He might not know me like a friend anymore, but he knows me better than most people ever could. It's the consequence of growing up together.

Tamara is exactly my type, or rather—the *Daly* type. Busty, curvy, and hot enough to model. All of us have a string of hotties in our collective pasts, and Tamara is no different.

So he's not wrong about Kinsley. Because she isn't my type.

I just can't figure out why that bothers me.

When we make it to the docks, we take turns tooling around on the two Jet Skis my parents have. Thankfully, we manage to share for the few hours we're out on the water, taking turns like good boys. The water washes away my concerns, as it always does, the best salve known to mankind.

The afternoon melts away in summertime bliss. Sunlight so pure, it makes me squint, even with sunglasses on. The rhythmic crash of waves against the wooden dock posts as I watch Mav stand on the Jet Ski out on the water, sending spray behind him in a graceful arc. And the gulls, circling nearby, which remind me of the incident with Kinsley the other day. That puts the perma-grin back on my face.

Once we make the trek home and Mom is starting dinner, Kinsley still hasn't texted. I've got some time to kill, and I'm starting to feel restless, so I head to the bedroom and pull out my laptop. Code hard or die, basically. I lose myself in my project easily; the time away from it has given me a new perspective.

And yes, I'm coding on vacation again. But the sooner I finish this, the better. The raw tension of being stuck in a stagnant career pond is potent enough to gnaw through my feel-good vibes here in Bayshore. Once this is done, I'll have direction again.

My phone buzzes in the middle of my code-a-thon. An hour has melted by, and I barely noticed. Mom has texted to say dinner is in five. I log onto social media, one of the few times I've even gotten on my account since hitting Bayshore.

And of course, the first thing that pops up is Tamara. She went to some bridal shower, and she's showcasing one of her infamous selfies with mauve fish lips and overflowing cleavage. Seeing her reminds me of one of the prime directives of my trip: piss her off.

Originally I thought the trickle-down of news after the fact might be satisfactory, but a new idea occurs to me in a flash. I swipe through my phone and pick the best selfie of Kinsley and me from the other day. No caption. No explanation. Just two happy, ruddy-faced people who are probably fucking, enjoying Bayshore and life and each other.

Before I post, I edit one important detail. The audience. This is a bitchfest-inducing, jealousy-inspiring mission, so my tactic only needs to reach one demographic.

Tamara.

# CHAPTER FIFTEEN

KINSLEY

I stay away from the Daly household for as long as I can stand it. Because I don't know how to move forward from here.

Every bit of my innards are screaming for *more more more*. More sex, more Connor, more of this fun and flirty connection we've unwittingly stumbled upon. But the more I think about it, the more confused I get.

Because this is fake—right?

And if it's fake, it won't go anywhere. Even though, if I listen hard enough, I can hear wedding bells in the distance. I should enjoy it for what it is, which is an entirely unclear and befuddling situation that we've created ourselves. Reap the orgasms while they're ripe, which is a saying that no one has said ever.

But around eight p.m., I'm feeling the itch for more Connor. I need to face the music. We need to figure out how to address the fact that we had an intimate slip, a cascade of carnality. Because I know the truth: it's just sex for Connor. I'm a warm body in the same bed.

He wouldn't look twice at me if he had his pick of all the women in Bayshore, and I repeat this to myself as I text him.

*KINSLEY: Ready for me?*

*CONNOR: You have no idea. Where should I meet you?*

Butterflies swarm to life in my belly. He's probably stressed from spending the day with his brothers, but it's nice to think that maybe he missed me. I seriously need to stop indulging in this sort of fantasy, though. It's only going to hurt me later.

*KINSLEY: Pick me up at High-5's?*

It's a neutral middle ground between my parents' house and his. He tells me to give him ten minutes, so I say goodbye to my parents and start the late evening walk to the locally famous bar.

When I get there, I stop at the back of the deck behind High-5's. It overlooks the grassy knoll that slopes down the side of the bar toward the boardwalk below. Boats are docked all along the shore here—it's the convenient hitching post for boaters when they need to stop downtown to grab a bite to eat or a beer.

Connor is coming down the boardwalk toward High-5's, his hands shoved into the pockets of his light-gray shorts. He's wearing a blue and white striped muscle shirt, and the sight of his casual saunter makes my core tighten immediately.

This man was *inside me* roughly twelve hours ago. A shiver trembles up my spine, and for a moment, all I can do is stare at him and recall the moment when he first pushed himself inside me. Will I ever recover from that? Or will ten years go by, and I'll still be held hostage by the memory of his perfect cock while I'm stuck in a dissatisfying relationship with someone who isn't Connor?

"Kinsley!"

His gruff voice snaps me out of my reverie. He's climbing the cement steps that cut through the sloping knoll up to the back patio. I'm white knuckling the railing of the patio, and it takes me a moment to find my voice.

"Hi, Connor." I tuck some hair behind my ear, swallowing hard as he heads toward me. A million thoughts collide inside me. Light-hearted quips and casual comments that might mask my nervousness fight for airtime on my tongue. I try to force some combination of them together. "What's you?"

A grin curls his lips, and he slows to a stop in front of me. I replay my words in my head, and I pinch my eyes shut.

"What?"

I press the heel of my hand to my forehead. "I mean...how are you? Or, what's up...I don't know. Hi." I offer my hand, which he takes cautiously. "I'm Kinsley, the biggest dork on the planet. Pleased to meet you."

His grin widens as we shake hands. "I wouldn't say *biggest...*"

"Oh, no?"

"Definitely top five." Our hands drop slightly, and I swear he squeezes mine before he lets go.

I snicker while humiliation rises up like a phoenix inside me. "Well, I'm ready when you are. Do with me what you will."

His eyebrow lifts. People are milling around us, drinks in hand, but this isn't primetime for this spot yet. After nine, the bands start, and this back patio gets packed shoulder to shoulder. But for now, there's still room to breathe.

"Want to grab a drink first?"

I expel a breath I didn't realize I was holding. "Yes, actually."

This sense of direction is helpful. We're getting a drink. That might take the edge off this nervousness that has flared up like the newest strain of influenza. Everything that has come out of my mouth so far has been slightly off. I don't have much hope for all the words yet to escape.

I don't know how to *be* around Connor now that we've had sex.

I follow his broad shoulders as we weave inside High-5's, through laughing groups of friends and couples clinking glasses of wine. He finds a bartender and is already ordering when I reach the edge of the bar beside him. The bartender flits away before I can say anything.

"Did you order for me, too?"

He nods, sending me a mysterious smile. I try to see what the bartender is preparing, but it's impossible. My belly flutters.

"What did you get?" I ask.

"You'll see," he says, and then leans against the bar, elbows behind him. "Just something to enjoy the sunset."

I squash the silly grin which threatens to take over my face. Because this is still acting. Even though we're away from the family, he probably still wants to be able to say, "Kinsley and I spent a romantic evening watching the sunset." So this is all part of the ruse. He's not buying me a drink because he really wants to.

It's so hard to keep my footing in all of this. But I forget the grapple when the drinks arrive. Two RumChatas. I find his gaze waiting for mine, laughter in his eyes.

"You didn't."

"Cheers, Kins." He lifts his tumbler and clinks it against mine. We both take a long sip, and he pays the bartender. A moment later, he coughs. "Been a long time since I've had one of these."

"Probably since senior year of high school, right?"

A laugh crinkles his eyes again. "Actually, yeah."

The moment settles pleasantly between us. I forget about my confusion, about my nervousness. But only briefly. As he leads us out of the bar and back toward the patio, where sunset has exploded in a raucous, golden volcano of light and sunbeams, all of my tension returns. Do I act like we didn't fuck? Was that lovemaking or something else? Can Connor be considered a hookup now?

He heads toward a tall table along the wooden railing. We slide onto the stools, and I offer a smile.

"How was your day?"

God, this feels so formal, which is even more embarrassing. I want to crawl into a hole somewhere. I jerk my gaze from the table and out toward the lake. Better to concentrate on the orange and red hues rippling across the bay. That makes way more sense than what's going on between us right now.

"It was awesome. My mom and I went to the mall. She bought me some new underwear. Now I have a new pair for every day of the week."

"So you have the complete granny-panty collection?"

His words make my eyes go wide. I look over at him and see the shit-eating grin on his face. My cheeks flame instantly, and I down half of my RumChata. This, right here? This is what I've been afraid of. I'm not on his level. He's used to confident women in thongs that double as dental floss. I'm just a lost girl in granny panties that double as wash rags.

When I don't respond, he adds, "They're cute. I like them."

I groan, covering my face with my hands.

"And I haven't even seen the new ones yet. But I'll probably like those, too."

I nibble on my lips, shaking my head. "Don't worry. I won't make you suffer through that."

He grabs my wrist then, tipping his chin so that his gaze finds mine, heated and intense. "I don't think you understand what I'm saying, Kins. I *want* to see the new ones."

My cheeks flame again, but not from embarrassment this time. I look away from him, because meeting his gaze sparks too much confusion. Somewhere deep down, I know this is a game for him.

His stool scrapes over the wooden slats of the deck as he scoots closer to me. His arm brushes against me as he leans in close.

"Was this morning a dream, or did I fuck you so hard that you fell asleep on top of my dick?"

I wince, even though his words are so sexy, I feel a lick of arousal run through me. God, he probably thinks I'm such a little girl. I can't hold my own against a man like him. I fell asleep while he was still inside me, for God's sake. "I think we both agreed at the start that we were dreaming."

He clears his throat, glancing around before leaning in so close that his lips brush my ear. "Then I think we should go back to dreamland."

My entire face is in flames. It has to be, because this man's words are too hot for me to properly comprehend. This isn't just half-awake bodies next to each other in bed. He's sober and awake and actually *saying this*. I dare myself to look up at him, and it takes all my strength. As much as I'm turned on by him, I'm also languishing from embarrassment. I'm not a sexy goddess. I'm no man's fantasy. I learned that over and over again from my ex. Which means that whatever Connor is responding to now is based on pure testosterone.

He just wants to have sex. And so do I. Even though I also want so much more.

I muster up my huskiest voice. "Finish your RumChata."

A grin spreads across his face, the type that involves dimples and sparkling irises, and I fall a little bit deeper in love with him. I could look at his face for a full year, strapped to one chair, no blinking involved, and still want more. *Another thing to not say out loud, Kinsley!*

He finishes the rest of his drink in a gulp, and I attempt the same. It takes me two and a half swigs. I wipe my mouth, and we slide off the stools. He grabs my hand, our footsteps thudding across the deck as he leads me toward the stairs and down to the boardwalk.

It's hard to hide the silly smile on my face. It's hard not to get swept up in dreamy what-ifs. This, right here—this is the confusing shit. It feels so real, but I know it can't be.

But even so, I giggle while he tugs on me to hurry behind him, only to stop abruptly to point out a cawing group of seagulls.

"They're still displeased," Connor says, faux-serious.

"What's the reason this time?"

"Because you stayed away so long today." Connor squeezes my hand, resuming the quick pace from before. His words repeat a few times in my head, and I fight back the warm fuzzies as best I can. The boardwalk curves around the bayfront, and by the time we're hitting the northeastern lip of his parent's neighborhood, the sunset turns bloated and brilliant. We pause, gasping and pointing, as the fat, red ball sinks beneath the horizon.

The wispy clouds in the sky turn fuchsia and violet as the sun's effects continue to dance across the heavens. Seeing something like that sends a whoosh of prickly energy through me. My entire body is tingling with excitement, and that has as much to do with Connor's big hand around mine as the hot-pink skyline.

We cross into the neighborhood, sand tracked over the first few feet of asphalt road as we snag the uneven sidewalk leading down the street. He hasn't explicitly said it, but I'm fairly sure we're going to have sex as soon as we set foot in his parents' house. We might even half undress as we stumble up the staircase. At least, that's what I'm hoping.

He glances back at me. "What color are they?"

"What?"

"Your new collection."

Amusement ripples through me. "Oh, a variety. Deep purple. One is sky blue. Another pair is white stripes with like, pink edging..." I slow my pace beside him. "Actually, I have them here. Do you want to see them?"

His grip tightens around my hand. "Not yet. We don't want to be indecent on the sidewalk."

The neighborhood is bustling with activity at this time of night. I always liked this neighborhood growing up, because it seemed so tight-knit and funky. That aspect hasn't changed a bit. A younger couple is dragging out the wooden boards to set up cornhole on their driveway as we walk past. The next house over, an older man is fighting with a tiki torch, and he mutters, "I'm ready to tiki *torch* this thing," as we walk by.

Connor's parents' house is about a block and a half away. As we curve down the road, pointing out interesting flowers and lawn decorations to each other, a shout stops us.

"Connor Daly! Get your ass over here!"

A guy our age is waving at us from inside an open two-car garage. People are milling around inside, and I realize we're staring at Adam Schmidt from high school.

"Adam! Get the hell out." Connor heads toward his old friend, and the two give each other a bro-hug. I do a quick scan of the scene, and there aren't too many other faces I recognize. I smile politely as Connor and Adam exchange pleasantries. Connor gestures toward me.

"You remember Kinsley, right? Kinsley Cabana."

"Hey, Adam." I wave.

"Yeah, of course. Man, what a reunion. You two want a beer?" Adam ushers us into the garage, where it's a whole spread of summertime fun. Cornhole boards are stacked off to the side, right beside the wall of life jackets and pool toys. In the middle of the garage, two big tables are set up: one for beer pong, where a blonde girl is laying out the cups, and another one for ping-pong.

"Yeah, I'll take one." Connor points at me. "You too, babe?"

Stars explode in my eyes. He called me *babe* in public. We don't have to convince these people, but we are anyway. "Uh, yeah. Sounds great."

Adam grabs two beers from a nearby cooler and launches into conversation. He's here for the summer, on break from the school in Indiana where he teaches. He's been doing that the past few years—working all year in Indiana, spending two solid months in Bayshore. Everyone around us agrees it's the life.

I sip nervously at my beer, wondering who I might be able to strike up a conversation with. I need to prove to Connor, and myself, that I am not a lame addition here. I want to be someone that can confidently attend a party. Someone that others are excited to see. Someone that Connor might be happy to show off.

*Connor will never be showing you off. You seriously need to stop thinking like this.*

While Connor and Adam catch up, I smile and nod and accidentally down my whole beer. Once I toss it, Adam blinks at me.

"Let me get you another."

"Damn, girl," Connor says, nudging me.

"Just thirsty, I guess." I laugh weakly, but the little buzz from the RumChata and the beer is helpful. I feel a little looser. I feel like I can *do this.*

Adam comes back with another beer. "Thanks, man," I say, cracking it open. "Appreciate it." Adam and Connor start chatting again, and I find my mark. The brunette nearby with a crop top and an eyebrow ring. I drift her way, waving.

"Hey, there. I'm Kinsley. What's your name?"

She tips her head to the side, like maybe I'm speaking a foreign language. "Winnie?"

"No, Kinsley. With a K."

"But I'm Winnie."

"Oh." I slap my forehead. "Right. Winnie. Nice to meet you." This is not going well so far. I feel like it's been three years since I last willingly put myself in a social situation with strangers that weren't the coffee shop baristas near my workplace. "So...do you have a dog?"

Holy hell. That's my only conversation starter? *Do you have a dog?* I'm melting from exasperation on the inside while she snickers.

"No. Just a parrot."

"A freaking parrot? Really?" This is genuinely amazing. "Can I see a picture of it?"

Winnie reaches for her phone while I stew about how awkward I am. Beer doesn't help—nothing helps. I glance back at Connor, and we lock eyes across the garage. Somehow, the brief connection is bolstering. After Winnie shows me her parrot, we launch into a real conversation. She just graduated from college and has no idea what to do next. She got a business degree—same as me—but feels so uninspired by the options out there.

We fall face forward into what can only be called a gabfest. My second beer goes untouched as we moan and groan about the annoying aspects of career fairs and how silly the mock interviews tend to be. She wants to move out west but doesn't know where. I tell her Connor and I can help, and then he and Adam eventually join the conversation.

Time melts away. Some of the other people at Adam's house flit in and out. Behind us, someone begins a ping-pong match.

"Oooh," I say, watching as two young guys bat the ball back and forth. "I love ping-pong."

"You want next?" one of them asks me.

"Mm hmm." I set down my now-warm beer, mesmerized by the back and forth. Nobody knows it yet, but ping-pong is *my thing*. I endure their match until one of them hands over a paddle.

And then the beat-down begins. I don't know why, but God blessed me with mad ping-pong skills. It could have been physical beauty, conversational grace, or unabashed style sense, but no. It's ping-pong skills.

But I work with what I've got. And I absolutely destroy the gangly guy in front of me named Derek or Wilber or whatever; I was too busy focusing on my game to catch his name. Everyone at the party gathers around to watch. I punctuate each point with a karate chop on the table. In times like these, slightly buzzed and feeling mildly successful, I wonder if I could make a career out of ping-pong.

Someone takes video, and I'm pretty sure there's at least one potential meme somewhere in the photos that Connor got of me. But finally, after over an hour of drinking and cheering and ponging, Connor wraps an arm around my waist and his hot breath appears at my ear.

"Kins, let's go."

I drop my paddle without a second thought.

# CHAPTER SIXTEEN

CONNOR

Mom and Grayson are in the backyard when we get back to the house, but we don't stop to say hi. We don't stop for anything. I lead Kinsley up the staircase, her hand clamped in mine lest she go off to make a new best friend or wow the world with her ping-pong skills again.

Don't get me wrong. Both are very good qualities for a girl to have. I just need her in our bedroom, *now*.

The door clicks shut behind us. I turn on the lamp beside the bed, and she watches me with doe eyes. There's something so innocent about her. Like she's never done this before, even though she has. And as always, her gaze only meets mine for a moment before it falls elsewhere. I can't get enough of that periwinkle. She's gnawing on her lip, waiting for me to make a move.

"Okay. Let's see them." I jerk my chin toward the bed. "Granny panty collection."

She laughs, dropping her big purse on the bed. "Seriously?"

She has no idea how serious I am. It's like she doesn't know how hot she is. "Lay 'em out."

She rolls her lips inward while she digs around in her purse. Personally, I would have loved to go shopping for these panties *with her*, but maybe that's for the future. The bag crinkles as she tugs out seven pairs of new panties. She sets her purse on the floor and then lays them out side by side. Fuchsia, pitch black, sky blue, yellow stars on red, and more. She sends me a coy look.

"These." I snag the fuchsia pair, then push all the rest off the bed. "Let's see these."

She's nibbling on her lip again. "You really...?"

I nod, and she heads for the bathroom.

"Where are you going?" I call out before she shuts the door.

"To put these on."

"Kins." I laugh at the innocence of it. "You don't want to change out here?"

"I mean..."

My cock twitches while urgency pumps through me. I want her on top of me already. I want her unraveling in my arms. "Come in here and take your clothes off."

Understanding flashes in her eyes. She cocks a smirk and heads my way again.

"You want a strip tease." She pulls down the shoulder of her loose shirt. I nod, letting the grin on my face say it all. "Even though this will be the worst strip tease in all of history?" she asks, and then tugs off her shirt in one swift movement.

Her small breasts are encased in a black satin bra. I'm fully hard thinking about putting my lips around one of those pink nipples.

"It's going pretty well so far," I say, adjusting my junk so the waistband of my pants doesn't sever my dick. Her gaze drops to my crotch, and a smile curls her lips.

Kinsley unbuttons her striped shorts and pushes them to the ground. She's wearing black boy short underwear, which she also pushes down a moment later. I grit my teeth as my gaze falls over the tight patch of hair covering her pussy. I want to run a finger over those lips, followed by my tongue, followed by my cock. One morning with her, and I love her pussy, I know this already.

I suck at my bottom lip as she reaches for the fuchsia panties.

"Take your bra off," I say, my voice a little husky.

"You take your shorts off," she counters.

Fair enough. I fumble with the drawstring and push them down over my bulging briefs. Once they're discarded on the floor, she unhooks her bra. It crumples to the ground, exposing her pert breasts and those rosy pebbles that I'm already desperate to bite.

Kinsley is long lines and slight curves. She's like a fancy exclamation point. I would tell her this if I wasn't so turned on right now and could form words.

Her gaze finds mine, pure heat and vulnerability there. "Take your shirt off."

I tear it off in record time, tossing it to join my shorts on the floor. She steps into the fuchsia panties, and they rise up just below her tanned hipbone. Beautiful.

Now they need to come off.

"Come here."

She steps forward, and I snag her as soon as she gets close. Her skin is silky warmth against mine as she falls forward. We tumble backwards onto the bed, her breasts smashed against my chest. We laugh, but then the kissing begins. Urgent kisses laced with tenderness. Not like this morning, which was exploratory eroticism in a dreamworld. Now, we're alert. Now, we *know* what awaits us.

She moans through a kiss, and I push my palms along the line of her thigh, up and over the swell of her ass cheeks. She tastes like vanilla and beer, a heady combination that makes my cock ache. I don't just want her. I *need* her.

I massage her perfect little ass cheeks, my fingertips dipping beneath the fabric of her new panties. She inhales sharply. I urge her legs open, and she sits on top of me, my trapped cock tenting my briefs between us.

"Do you like them?" she asks.

"You tell me." I thrust my hips, showing off how much I'm a fan.

She giggles. "They're basic cotton underwear. Because I'm a basic cotton girl."

"Pff." I cup her breasts, running my thumbs over the tight points of her nipples. A shiver wracks her body and her eyes go hooded. "How do you want it, Kins?"

"Want what?" she asks, her voice a million miles away.

"When I fuck you."

Her eyes snap open, round and shocked. God, her innocence is cute. And I'm not even talking dirty.

"Whatever...I don't know...you tell me."

I tut, shaking my head. I thrust my hips again, generating some friction between our groins as her fuchsia-covered pussy rubs up against my black-tented cock. "You pick."

She gulps, her gaze falling over my shoulders, then down the flat expanse of my abs. She seems hesitant to speak. Like maybe she's never been asked this before.

"In the shower?" she squeaks.

Fine by me. I swipe my thumb over each nipple again, enjoying the way her head tips back and her expression melts into pure pleasure. I move my hands to her hips next, rubbing my fingertips back and forth over the crotch of her panties. A teasing move, one that makes her breath hitch.

"Your wish is my command." I almost call her *babe* again, but I stop myself. It always slips out—it's way too easy with her. I sit up, urging her to stand before I rummage in the nightstand for my only spare condom. I could hit up Mav for more, but really, I should go buy a huge pack for myself. We've still got a week and a half left, and I don't see this slowing down.

She scampers into the bathroom, and the water flips on. I follow behind her like a sex-seeking zombie. There's a stand-up shower in there, snug but adequate. It'll do, at least. She pushes her panties down and steps out of them, testing the water with her hand before she slips under the stream. Her hair is still in a loose braid behind her, but she's taken the hair tie off again. Anticipation thrills through me. My fingers twitch with the urge to expedite her hair reveal. It's just hair—I've never cared so much about any ex's tresses before. But with Kinsley, it's different. Like her hair is a secret she keeps, knotted up, reserved for a very select few.

I step out of my briefs, fisting myself as my gaze scorches over her lithe, naked frame, already dripping wet in the shower. I wet my bottom lip, tearing open the condom package before I get lost in there. Her gaze sizzles on me as I roll it over my cock.

Inside the shower, I cup her face in my hands, and we kiss, over and over again, under the stream of water. The taste of her gets diluted; our lips slip and our bodies slide against each other. And then I push her back against the wall. Hair has stuck to the side of her face as I kiss my way over her jawline and down her neck. I hoist her thigh up to my hip, my cock already seeking the one place it knows best.

Kinsley wraps her arms around my neck, arching toward me. I bury myself in the sweet hollow of her neck before I hoist her against the wall. Effortlessly, like she's a bird and her bones are hollow. A quirky bird. Another nickname for Sunny-kins. And the thought sounds like something she would say, which is even more amusing.

"What's so funny?"

I didn't realize I was laughing. I meet her gaze guiltily. "Nothing."

"You were snickering."

"I was just thinking about how you're so light." I press my abs against her belly. My cock strains to find the warm core of her. "Like your bones are hollow."

She laughs. "If they were, you bet your ass I'd be putting that on my resume."

We kiss through laughter, and then I'm easing myself inside her so slowly, our laughs turn into groans. She is stretching velvet around me. Even after our marathon morning, her pussy is a slick vice, and my whole body goes tense from the sensations.

"Ohhh, my God," she whispers into my ear. I'm still easing myself in, inch by groaning inch. Finally, I've buried myself to the hilt. Her thighs are rock hard around me, heels digging into my ass. I flex once and she moans.

"Fuck." I drag my teeth along her jawline for a moment. Like a way to pace myself and get my bearings. "You feel so good, Kinsley."

"I know. I know. I knooow." She arches against me, the water skimming the tops of her breasts. Jesus, she looks so sexy right now. Water trickling down over her rib cage, blonde hair plastered to her chin. My biceps are bulging from the way I'm holding her, her ass in my hands so I can control the slow, measured pace I'm inflicting on both of us. It's a torturous version of paradise.

I rock against her once, then again. Each time I push into her, her belly caves in and her pussy clamps down around me. This girl is working with me, that's for sure. But she's a little too good at what she does. I might have come hours ago, but my entire body is vibrating, tense and eager to dive into another orgasm. I dip my head down and take one of Kinsley's nipples between my teeth, laving my tongue against the pebbled tip. She moans and bucks against me.

"Be careful," she hisses.

"Of what?"

"Of making me cooome." She arches again, eyes pinched shut.

"Isn't that the point?" I smile as I move my tongue to the other breast.

"Yes, but"—a breath huffs out of her—"not this *fast*."

So she wants this to last as much as I do. And maybe we'll get there, *someday*, but not today. I know because she's already digging her nails into the tops of my shoulders. I know because she's started doing that cute whimper noise, the one caught halfway between having a bad dream and the best orgasm of your life.

I ease back into her again, faster this time. She groans low.

Fuck it. We're not gonna last much longer; let's go for the gold.

"Look at me."

She whimpers again, peering at me through hazy slits.

"I'm gonna go hard." I warn her because she's slight and I'm big. But she's going to lap this up like fucking honey. "And you're going to come even harder."

A smile ghosts her lips, and she nods. I brush my lips against hers.

"Ready?"

"Do me."

I laugh, but it fades quickly. I squeeze her apple ass cheeks and steel myself. I push into her again, iron into velvet, tension giving way to passion. I fuck her—*hard*—but not like a maniac. Like a measured pro, a man who wants her to enjoy this every bit as much as I do.

But there's power here. A lot of it. Our bodies are colliding in a rhythm that transcends melody. This is fucking perfection. We're banging against the shower wall, a noise I register distantly but can't care about. She's too warm, too soft, too tight to give a damn about anything else.

I hoist her again, and my cock angles deeper inside of her. Then suddenly she's crying out, absolutely screaming and clawing at the tiled wall, and her pussy turns into a vice. She pulls me over the edge with her, and I slip into the abyss right after her, freefalling and fluid, the heat pumping so fast through my veins that I think I go legally blind for a second.

I fuck her until I can't anymore, until the condom is full and my dick starts to go soft. She's whimpering and writhing and moaning my name. I ease out of her, but I don't put her down.

Instead, I press a kiss to her forehead.

And then another.

Finally, our eyes lock.

And this time, she lets me look into that periwinkle paradise for as long as I like.

# CHAPTER SEVENTEEN



Thirteen years have gone by in the domestic bliss bubble that we've created in Connor's parents' house. Okay, okay—maybe it's more like thirty-six hours. But damn, it feels so much longer.

Like we've been doing this for eons. How strange it is to fall into a rhythm like this with a relative stranger. Even though we're no longer strangers, a week ago, we *were*. And now, we're waking up at nine each morning and having oatmeal together. Sharing the newspaper and commenting on politics and staring out the sliding door into the backyard to see which birds we can identify.

And honestly, my life before Connor has almost faded into distant memory. This jaunt—whatever it really is—has been a much-needed respite from my underwhelming work and social life back in San Diego. I love waking up beside him. I love giggling over sudoku after breakfast. I love all the sex, which is hands down the best I've ever had in my entire freaking life. Not like he had much competition, but I'm also positive he will continue to reign supreme if, for some reason, I decide to shack up with anyone else.

But I probably will, I remind myself. Because Connor is not The One. He is *posing* as The One. And damn, he does a good job at it.

So good that he's even fooling me. The man picks out my underwear each morning, for God's sake. How am I supposed to not let that sway me? He has a vested interest in my plain panties, which speaks volumes about him.

Apparently my sixteen-year-old self-picked a good one. Because Connor was my dream man then and still is now.

The more I get to know him, the more I want him forever.

Which means that having only one week left with him is cuing the panic.

As if I haven't been confused and anxious about all this enough. I do a good job hiding my anxiety via nervous jokes and staring off into the distance, imagining ten million improbable outcomes for any given situation. So it's not like I think Connor *knows* I'm a nervous wreck about this la-la-land fantasy coming to an end.

I really enjoy our slow mornings together, and the way he'll randomly pull up the picture with the seagull zoomed in right on the angry bird face. I haven't laughed this much since college, when I lived around my friends constantly. Honestly, Connor would have fit right in with my group.

He fits in with me in a *lot* of ways, I'm finding.

But when I find him set up on his laptop in the breakfast nook the following Wednesday after breakfast, I remember that for all the ways we fit together in Bayshore, he still has a whole other life in San Diego that I know nothing about.

I sit next to him, running a comb through my freshly washed hair. "Whatcha doing?"

He glances at me over the top of his black-rimmed glasses that are both hipster and elderly. "Guess."

"Coding."

He shoots me a thumbs up. "Except not just that. I'm *finishing* coding."

"You mean you're quitting?"

He expels a frustrated noise. We haven't talked much about work while we've been back home—okay, we haven't talked about it *at all*—but that one noise catches me up on all I need to know about his position at E-bid.

"That's what this app is going to help me do. Get out of E-bid. I'll never quit coding, though."

I tug my comb through some tangled strands at the ends. Tiny droplets occasionally flick his way.

"I thought you liked it at E-bid," I say.

He grimaces. "I do. But it's just…" He glances around, like checking for eavesdroppers. "There's nowhere else for me to go there. I've maxed out, and I don't want my boss's job. I need something better."

I nod, focusing on the black comb I'm pulling through my long strands. "Yeah. I feel the same way."

Curiosity spikes in the air between us. That's another thing we haven't talked about at all—Tamara. It's not like I've forgotten that they used to date and she's my boss. It's been easy enough to overlook in the hullabaloo of being back in Bayshore.

When his gaze meets mine, questions dance there, though he says nothing.

"I don't want to badmouth her," I add. "She's…not what I expected."

"Who?"

"You know who."

Connor clears his throat, gnawing on the inside of his cheek. His gaze flits back to the laptop, and he clicks his mouse randomly for a moment. "Does she give you trouble?"

"That would be putting it nicely."

His fingers tap on the keyboard and my hair goes *swish* as the comb swipes through. "What does she do?"

I sigh, pausing in my combing. The laundry list is honestly so long. But half of the items might sound like I'm paranoid or complaining, even though I *know* that Tamara is out to get me somehow. I haven't been able to put my finger on it yet, though.

"You know how some people have this constant, underlying sense of dread or doom that someone's going to die or get in a plane crash or make their life awful?"

Connor nods.

"Well, that's how I feel about Tamara. There's something about her that I don't trust. Nothing has played out yet, but I'm still not convinced it won't."

Connor squints at me. "So you're nervous about losing your job?"

"It's not that. Every time I have a suggestion or policy modification or process tweak, she finds at least ten reasons why that idea is completely unactionable or useless. And I'm really bringing my A game here." The words are tumbling out of me. "I showed up at E-bid ready to make things better. To, I don't know, *shine* or something. But there are roadblocks at every turn. I can't make any progress."

He huffs. "Sounds familiar."

Our shared experience is only minimally comforting, though. Sure, we can commiserate. But what's the next step?

"Yeah. Sounds like we need to find new jobs," I finally say.

"Hopefully this app will get me there." He pauses, his eyes darting back and forth over the tabletop. "Are you sure you really want to be in HR?"

"I love the atmosphere. I love the work involved. I just wish..." I shake my head, wondering how much more I should complain about his ex to his face. He hasn't given me any sign that he agrees with me. Hell, he hasn't given me one iota of information about her, and I'm too chickenshit to ask. So I guess we'll keep avoiding it. "I wish I had Tamara's job. I think I could do it better."

"In what ways?"

"My interactions with people aren't fraught with power plays." Jeez, the dirt is spilling out now. I couldn't stop it if I tried. "I don't emotionally manipulate people. Just for starters."

"Why don't you tell me how you really feel?"

A laugh escapes me. "Yeah. Well. You're getting the brunt of it, because I don't really have anyone else to tell. Tamara would be the person, except she's also the problem."

Connor leans back in the wooden chair, which creaks as he brings his palms behind his head. "I think the whole structure is messed up at E-bid. I have a list of a hundred things I would change."

"Same here."

Silence settles between us. When Connor finally looks over at me, he says, "So where would you go if you had your pick?"

A sigh billows out of me. I resume combing my hair. "Honestly? I have no idea."

"You don't have a dream job?"

"I do, but it's not...available, I guess. It's more of a concept."

He narrows his eyes at me. "Explain."

"I don't know. I want something creative within the formality of the business world. I feel like Tamara doesn't respond well to my creative ideas. She wants the black and white, nine to five, so she can clock out and say she did her job. But so much more could be done if she'd give a damn and think outside the box. I've presented so many efficiencies, so many new approaches, so many projects that would solve the redundancy and bitch work. But it goes unnoticed, unutilized. And if that's how the corporate world is, I don't know what company is going to accept me like I am."

I'm aware of how much I'm complaining about my job, but hell if I can shut up now. Besides, there's something sexy about Connor's thoughtful questions and the fact that he's really listening to me.

"And truthfully? I'm not inspired to start a job hunt only to find out that the next job has me in the same position as this one."

Connor nods. "Yeah. I'm right there with you. So we should start our *own* businesses."

I snort. "Sure. In what? You have plenty of options. But in the HR world, I'm so green, I couldn't even convince a college student to hire me as a tutor."

Connor inspects his hands as he runs his thumb over his knuckles. "Right. But you've been in a professional environment for two years. You have the drive. You have the creativity. That makes up for the other areas you might not be as well-developed in."

I toss the comb on the table. "All right. Find me the job and tell me where to apply."

His grin goes ear to ear. "You know, as an app developer, I take that as a challenge."

"Good. Make me the app that tells me which is the right risk to take. Because honestly? I don't even know anymore. Let's make an algorithm figure it out. That's what they're good at, right?"

He snickers, but I'm only half joking. I would pay money at this point for a life coach to analyze my bullshit and tell me whether it's time to walk away from E-bid or I'm just being a flighty little jerk. Part of me wishes that I could blame my dissatisfaction on some sort of personality defect. *Standards too high. Must work harder at becoming satisfied with life's offerings.*

But the other part of me knows that something isn't right. And I'm not sure how much longer I can keep up the charade that I enjoy the corporate environment.

And at age twenty-five, this feels so overwhelming in a way that I never saw coming. I should be well on my way in my career by now, but instead, I'm single, unhappy, and stilted, with no idea how to fix things.

Worse yet, I hate myself for being unhappy, because I should have the world at my fingertips and relish it. So it's an anxiety cycle that accomplishes approximately nothing. Hence why I don't talk about it much.

Connor is the only one I've opened up to about it. I haven't even told my girlfriends yet, because they're all flying high in their careers. I don't want to bog them down with directionless malaise.

Footsteps scuff softly down the hallway, and Grayson appears a moment later. He's squinty-eyed and shirtless. "Hey, guys."

Connor makes a big display of checking his watch. "Musta been a late night."

"I was tearing up flooring until two a.m." Grayson yawns loudly as he stares into the fridge. "Which, by the way, if you're ever bored…"

Grayson started renovating the house he inherited from their grandmother while he's trying to sell it. I expect Connor to scoff and brush off his brother's comment, but he squints up at Grayson like he's thinking about it.

"You need help today?"

Grayson nods. "Yeah. I need help *every day*. Weston helped yesterday; I'm gonna rope Mav in too."

"I'm in." Connor turns to me, genuine excitement radiating off him. "You want to help too?"

His eagerness is endearing, but I can already sniff out that this is a sacred brother's project. The type of thing that the three of them just *need*. "No, I don't think so. I'm gonna go out on the lake with my mom today, but I'll be back for dinner."

Connor nods, searching my face for a moment. Then he leans forward and presses a kiss to my lips. "Promise?"

I'm toying with the tip of my braid, biting back the start of an impossibly huge grin. "Promise."

# CHAPTER EIGHTEEN

KINSLEY

My day on the boat with my mom leads to a ridiculous sunburn in the shape of an open book on my stomach. Because I'm that girl who falls asleep on the bow while reading *Into The Wild*. Apparently wilderness survival puts me to sleep.

At any rate, I'm hot and unevenly burnt when I head back to Connor's parent's house. He meets me outside, lifting the strap of my sundress.

"You look toasty."

"Yeah, yeah." I wave him off. "Another casualty of Bayshore summer sun."

He slides his hand over the small of my back as we go inside. His forearms look dusty, and that's when I notice he's wearing a t-shirt and dirty jean shorts. He's been working with Grayson all day, clearly. I head up the stairs, and he follows me wordlessly. Once we're in the bedroom and I'm dropping my things, he's got that look in his eyes. The one that says he's hungry.

*For me.*

"You gonna take a shower?" he asks.

"I thought I might rinse off." I can't hide the smirk. "Why, you want to fuck me against the shower wall again?"

His eyes go hooded. "Yeah, I thought that might be nice, actually."

My gaze washes over him. Dirt is streaked up his forearms, his knuckles are caked with who knows what. It's sexy, I can't lie. When he steps closer, I catch a whiff of his sweat-drenched scent. Hello, pheromones! I start sliding my sundress off immediately.

"That was fast," he murmurs.

"How can I resist you when you're all dirty and manly like this?" My sundress crumples to my feet, and I run my hands over the broad ridge of his shoulders. "What did you do today?"

"Fucked up some cupboards," he says, pressing his forehead to mine. "Painted some banisters." The scent of him steals my breath. Something raw and true sears through me: I never want to be without him.

But this isn't the time, and I'm probably being emotional. I bury the feelings, because they have no place here. Because I want to enjoy what few precious days we have left together here on this unexpectedly perfect vacation.

"Mmm. You want to paint *my* banister?"

He grins through a kiss. "That wasn't as sexy as you were intending it."

"Thanks for noticing."

He tugs at the tie of my bikini top until it releases, and the strings fall away behind me. He cups both of my cool—and very white—breasts in his hands while he coaxes a deep kiss from me. His thumbs make lazy swipes over my nipples, which prompts a gasp from me.

"You always go straight for the nips."

"Why wouldn't I?" His head dips and he sucks on one breast, hard. "You have the most perfect tits."

I must look as shocked as I feel on the inside, because he lifts a brow. "What's that look for?"

"Sorry. I can't believe you said that."

"Sorry. I can't believe you can't believe that." He swipes his middle finger along the curve of my breast, then down the bumpy ridges of my rib cage. "Have you looked at yourself?"

"I honestly try not to."

He glances sharply at me, which feels like a slap. "Kinsley."

"What? I'm a tall, skinny, awkward girl with barely-B's and no hips to speak of. I didn't luck out in the physical department." And it's true. I got the recessive Cabana gene. My sisters have bigger boobs and sharper dips in their waists than I do, a fact I always noticed once puberty hit. I kept waiting and waiting for my curves to appear, and then...surprise. They never showed. Like the worst ghosted date.

Connor sighs with frustration, guiding me back onto the bed. "Why is it so hard for you to believe that you're sexy?"

Emotion clamps my throat, and I focus on tracing the tip of my index finger along the grooves of his abs. It's because I dated a man who made sure I knew how frumpy and undesirable I was. Because growing up, when my older sister and I fought, her attack would always center on how ugly and tomboyish I was and how nobody would ever see past my weird ears and flat chest.

Because it fucking sucks being a woman sometimes, even though it can also be great.

Instead, I say, "Because you haven't submitted proper documentation for the Kinsley Board to review."

He snorts. "Fine. Here's your documentation." He bends my knees at his sides. "I'm going to make a note of every part of your body that has turned me on."

"In a twenty-four-hour period or all time?"

"All time." A cocky grin curls his lips. His hands grip my ankles. "Starting with here." He slides his hands up over my calves. "And here." He pushes the heel of his palm over my thighs, pausing to add, "And here."

"There are a lot of areas for the board to review."

"Mm-hmm." He pushes his hands beneath the fabric of my bathing suit bottoms, cupping my bare ass. "And all this back here." He squeezes my butt, then brings his hands to my hip bones. "And especially here."

I buck my hips as he smooths his hands back and forth over my mons, getting close to but not touching my most sensitive areas.

"This part right here, times a hundred."

He pushes his hands up my waist, squeezing my sides. His gaze falls to the obvious book-shaped white spot on my belly. "Oh, damn, what happened here?"

"I fell asleep with a book on my stomach." I cover my eyes with my hands.

A laugh meanders out of him as he assesses the area. "Weird tan line or not, this counts too."

"You get turned on by book-shaped whiteness?"

"Oh God, yes. And here." Then he cups my breasts. "Obviously here, but especially here." He pinches both my nipples at the same time.

I shriek, wriggling beneath him. "Not fair."

He comes onto his knees as he pushes his hands up over my chest and over my shoulders. "Also here." Then he runs his thumb over the outline of my lips. "And here, like, all the time." Then he pauses, staring into my eyes. "I'd poke your iris if I could, but I won't even attempt it."

"Thanks."

"And here." He smooths his hand over the top of my head, then all the way down to the tip of my braid.

"My braid?"

"Your brain, and also your hair."

I can't hide the grin anymore. I've never been so idolized. Still, it's hard for me to accept it. I want to move on. I know that this is only about sex for him. I'm fighting hard not to get disillusioned.

"You forgot to mention my wrists," I tease, clamping my thighs around him. I tug him close, so our groins connect. "You touched my wrist three times on the first night at the bar. So clearly, you're pretty attracted to it."

He laughs, but cloudiness enters his gaze. Maybe that was a weird comment. Maybe I shouldn't reveal that I counted how many times he touched my wrist.

"I guess I am." He buries his lips in the hollow of my neck. "So what does the Kinsley Board think of my presentation?"

"You'll be rewarded with entry."

His deep laugh makes my skin tingle. "Score."

He flips us over on the bed easily—hollow bones, after all—so that I'm on top and begins kissing a trail down my chest, between the valley of my too small breasts that he just called perfect. His tongue is dancing circles around the right nipple when Annette calls out from the hallway.

"Connor? Dinner's almost ready!"

He pauses, lips pressed to the side of my boob. Then a sigh escapes him.

"Okay, Mom, we're coming." He waits a moment, then sends me an apologetic look. "We should go downstairs. She made roast beef, corn casserole, and scalloped potatoes. If we don't, our German ancestors will turn in their graves."

We grumble and push off the bed, but not without stealing a few more kisses. I put on an actual bra and panties before slipping my sundress back over my shoulders. Connor follows me downstairs, and almost everyone has assembled. Damon is booming about something that happened at work that day, while Maverick fists the front of his hair and stares at his phone. Dom nods, listening to his dad with arms crossed over his chest. Weston is putting out forks while Annette counts dishes in the kitchen.

As usual, I dive into breaking the ice. "Let me help."

Annette doesn't really acknowledge me, per usual, but she doesn't say no either. She pushes a dish of scalloped potatoes my way. "This can go out."

I carry it out to the dining room table, setting the dish on top of a trivet that has a rabbit stitched into it. She glances at her phone and then hurries into the hallway, so I take it upon myself to carry out the remaining dishes.

While I'm helping arrange everything on the table, Connor takes his seat and falls into conversation with Weston about something they worked on at Grayson's house earlier that day. A few moments later, Annette bustles back into the kitchen, Grayson and another lady following behind her.

I recognize her immediately. Hazel Matheson. I only knew *of* her in high school, since she and Grayson were juniors to my freshman, but man, this babe turned buxom. She's fire-engine-red lipstick and winged eyeliner, part fifties, part modern-day pin-up. I blink dumbly.

*That's* the type of woman the Daly brothers attract.

And sure, Connor spent some time pointing out all the parts of my body that turned him on. But what I have to offer is not what he deserves long term. It might be fun for now, but what about when our Bayshore daydream is over? Maybe I should ask Hazel for some tips.

"Hi, Hazel. Remember me?" I wave as I arrange the last dish on the table. Grayson is all smiles. He's one hundred percent *not* the uptight prick I saw the first night in town.

We settle into our spots, and Annette glides right back into her practice of ignoring me while still availing herself of my helpfulness. And while Hazel is here, it's more than obvious how much she prefers Hazel over...well, probably her own sons. It's like she's already adopted Hazel as her daughter-in-law and is waiting for Grayson to make it official.

Really, it's kind of nauseating.

But maybe that's because I want Annette to talk to me like that, and realistically? She'll probably give me those frosty frowns until she's ninety-five and on a respirator.

I should take it as a warning sign. This isn't the family I want to marry into. Connor is not the guy for me. Yes, he might have commended my body parts earlier, but I can see what the Daly men are used to. They date Hazels, not Kinsleys. And the longer I fool myself with this strange are-we-aren't-we fake relationship, the harder it's going to be to pull myself out in a week.

Once dinner ends, Grayson and Hazel leave. Dom and his dad retire to the backyard for bourbon, and Mav and Weston head downtown for who knows what. Connor and I help Annette clean up, and his mom even says thank you. I'm so stunned, I can't speak, and in the clanking silverware and rush of the dishwasher, I begin to see the light at the end of the tunnel. Because the lightbulb has gone off.

Maybe things with Annette could change.

Maybe Connor isn't shitting me about being attracted to me.

Maybe I'm really my own worst enemy when it comes to believing in myself.

# CHAPTER NINETEEN

CONNOR

We're back in the bedroom later that night. Kinsley heaves a sigh as she tugs off her sundress. But it's not the sexy-time sort of clothes removal. It's the I'm-getting-ready-for-bed style of tossing her dress.

"Interesting that Grayson brought Hazel," I comment, unbuttoning my shorts. I'm watching her carefully. For a reaction. For a hint that she wants to finish what we started earlier. For basically anything.

"Yeah. I was under the impression they hated each other."

"So was everyone else." I tear off my work shirt and toss it onto the ground. I scratch my chest, watching as she busies herself organizing crap on the dresser that doesn't need her attention.

"They're cute together," she says.

"Yeah. I guess." I come up beside her, running a hand through my hair. It's grown a lot in the past week, seemingly, bordering on too long. I could use a cut, but I kind of dig the unkempt surfer look. "Hazel's not really my type though."

A disbelieving laugh rockets out of her. "You have to be kidding."

"Is that so hard to believe?"

"Hazel is a *goddess*."

I blink. "And...?"

"And I'm not."

Her words come down in the room like a sledgehammer. My brow furrows as I turn to her. But she won't meet my gaze. This, right here? This shit irritates me. When she avoids my gaze. It happened more in the beginning, but it still happens enough that I notice daily.

"Where did that come from?" I ask.

Kinsley sniffs, shrugging. "It's a fact. I mean look at her. She's beautiful. Grayson deserves someone like her. They would be the best power couple."

"Yeah, sure. If that's what you're into."

"Well, what are *you* into?"

It's a valid question, and one I don't have an answer for. I gnaw on the inside of my cheek as I watch her, waiting for her to meet my gaze.

"Kinsley," I finally say.

"What?"

"Look at me."

She does, for the briefest of seconds. Like a periwinkle fairy kiss, and then...she's back to focusing on anything else.

"Like, really look at me," I say and grab her by the arms, turning her toward me. She frowns a little, hazarding a glance or two my way. "You avoid my gaze. It's official. After a week living with you, I'm calling you out."

Her frown deepens. "What do you mean? I look at you all the time."

"Yeah, but not like this." I bend down, searching out her eyes. Her gaze ping-pongs across my face, down to my chin, and then finally, she looks right at me.

"Is this some sort of therapy technique?" she cracks.

"No. It's me trying to figure out why you won't make eye contact very often."

She blinks so much that I can feel the wind from her eyelashes. "I make eye contact."

"Not much." I hold her steady, so she won't bolt. This feels nice. And yeah, it does sorta feel like therapy. "And I think it has something to do with the fact that you don't believe your tits are perfect."

Her shoulders shake with laughter. "Oh, come on. You're not my therapist."

"Am I right?"

"I mean...maybe."

I release her, grinning because I'm onto something. "All right, so let's hear it."

"There's nothing to hear. I'm insecure like most every other woman in the world. Big deal."

She turns her attention to some discarded books near the dresser. The hard covers go *thud* as she stacks them in some system known only to her. I'm quiet, waiting for her to go on, but she says nothing. I can't force her to delve into something she doesn't want to. This was my way of bridging the remaining spaces between us. Once you're buried so deep in someone else, it's nice to get closer in an emotional sense.

But maybe she doesn't want that.

"If you don't want to go there, I won't bug you about it anymore," I finally say, flopping back on the bed.

One of the books goes *thwack*. "You really want to know?"

I fluff the pillow under my head. "I mean, I did ask."

*Thud.* "Fine. My ex kind of fucked me up. He was what you would call emotionally degrading." *Thunk.* "I don't tend to look people in the eye because I have a hard time believing anyone takes me seriously." *Fffwup.* "And if I look hard enough, there is evidence all around me of how pathetic I really am. So just invoice me what I owe you for the therapy session. I hope you accept Venmo."

I sit on her words for a little bit. Finally, I crane my neck to look down at her. She's sitting on her heels, books all around her, one stack to her left looking like it might topple at any second.

"You know you're fucking awesome, though, right?"

She sniffs, shrugging.

"Well, we're gonna work on this whole eye contact thing." When she doesn't acknowledge me, I squeeze the back of her neck. She shrugs my hand off, but I catch a grin on her face. "Because your eyes are gorgeous. And I really wish you'd look at me more."

Her hands freeze above the stack of books, and eventually, she turns to look at me.

"On a scale of one to ten," she begins.

I have no idea what the scale is measuring, but something in her tone tips me off. A grin blossoms on my face. "Easily eleven."

"Stop it," she says. "I didn't even clarify the terms."

"It doesn't matter. We both know what the scale is measuring." And yeah, we might be talking in cryptic vagueness that doesn't make a ton of sense. But with Kinsley, I get it. With Kinsley, I speak a different language. Our *own* language.

Weird how one week with her has provoked all of this.

Where will we be at the end of the second week? And what comes after that?

The thoughts feel heavier than I intend, which reminds me that I need a shower to wash it all away. I pinch her cheek and roll off the bed, heading for the bathroom. She doesn't join me, and I spend a long time under the warm stream, thinking about all the confusing strands of recent days that are threatening to tangle up into knots.

For how easy things feel with Kinsley, she also inspires a lot of questions. Questions that I'm not entirely sure how to answer.

I towel off in the bathroom, brush my teeth, and pad out into the bedroom sans underwear. Kinsley is in her sky-blue panties tonight, one knee bent as she reads a new book—the Chelsea Handler memoir. She's got on a basic gray tank top that hugs her slight curves. I step into a fresh pair of underwear and then climb onto the bed next to her.

But I'm not looking for sex. Well, not *this instant*, at least. There's something endearing about the way she's opened up to me, both tonight and this morning when we were complaining about our jobs. Call me sentimental, but I want to be with her. I've developed a soft spot for Kinsley in very little time.

I scoot toward her. "Need a pillow?"

She furrows her brow as if that's the silliest question she's ever gotten.

"Here." I gesture to my arms, and her mouth rounds. She scoots over to me, resting the back of her head on my chest, nuzzling into place for maximum comfort.

And when she beams up at me, gratitude and a lot more shining out of her, I feel a yank in my chest.

She doesn't have to say it. We're on the same page, and it feels more than right at her side.

# CHAPTER TWENTY



Time is running out, so I choose not to think about what happens Post-Bayshore.

We've got three days left before we head to Cleveland for our return flight to San Diego. It seems impossible, because time stops when I'm with Connor, therefore I should have an eternity left with him.

But after more ping-pong battles (I win them all) and nights with his brothers (Grayson is finally loosening up) and group renovations on their grandma's old house (the brothers are working together!), I decide that we need to do something special. A day-date of sorts.

So I arrange with my parents to borrow the boat one day while they're at work. I don't tell them who I'm taking or where I'm going, and they don't ask. I've grown up driving boats, so this isn't an odd request.

Connor and I clamber on board my parent's Sea Ray after lunch with a cooler full of beers and water bottles. I also brought some snacks, namely baby carrots and peanut butter and jelly sandwiches, and three books, even though I'm pretty sure I won't be reading at all on the lake today. I just need to be prepared *should* I choose to read.

But desperation laps at the edges of my composure, even though the sun beats down on us, and I've evenly applied my sunscreen this time, *just in case* I put a book across my stomach and fall asleep.

I guide the boat out of the marina downtown. Soon we're hitting white caps head on, the teal spray of lake water occasionally reaching us inside the boat. Connor sits in the bow, shirtless and laughing as we hit the waves. Each time he looks back at me, it makes my chest hurt a little.

I've been hemming and hawing about what to say to him. How I might ask if this real thing between us is actually real. Because even though he's been prodding at my insecurities, it doesn't mean they're gone. Now they're just...exposed. Quivering in the daylight, under his unyielding eye. Making it even harder to ask him what he might actually feel for me.

I've told Connor things that I never planned on sharing with anyone. But he still seems to enjoy being around me, even knowing that I have a hard time looking people in the eye because my self-esteem is shit and that I feel aimless in my adulthood. It's like he doesn't hold those things against me.

Which, in and of itself, is not a revolutionary concept. My girlfriends don't hold those things against me—well, they wouldn't, if they knew.

But my ex sure held stuff like that against me. My looks, most of all, but also any perceived sign of weakness or doubt. Sometimes he'd even rip me apart if I wasn't sure what I wanted for dinner. In his mind, things like that translated to glaring character defects that made me unfit to receive love.

And here's Connor, cruising along as if flaws can coexist with appreciation.

It's something I know deep down, but damn, it's been covered up by a lot of muck.

I head north into the wide, seemingly limitless expanse of choppy water. Sunlight glances off the surface of the water in the distance. Like a dolt, I forgot my sunglasses, so Connor lends me his spare pair. Because he's *that* cool that he always has two pairs. Wearing his sunglasses today feels about the same as an engagement ring, and there's something about the hot air and the splashing waves that dissolves every last bit of tension thrumming inside me.

I've never felt so alive. So fucking *happy*. I slow the boat down and guide it toward a relatively empty area of the bay around the thin strip of sand jutting out in the middle of the water. It's called the Sand Bar, and boaters love to congregate here, drop anchor, and have drinks between rounds of swimming out to the sandy embankment. It's in the middle of nowhere, a secret find of Briggs Bay. Connor helps me drop anchor, and then we collapse back into the seats of the bow.

"This day is so fucking beautiful!" he shouts as loudly as he can.

I laugh, propping my ankles on his lap. "Let's never leave."

"Live permanently in Briggs Bay?" He shrugs. "I'm down."

"Let's never leave *today*," I clarify. Because if time keeps moving forward, it will inevitably pull us apart.

"Okay. Time machine." He snaps his finger. "On it."

I smile over at him, the horizon behind him going askew then straight, askew then straight, as the boat is rocked by incoming waves. We lapse into a comfortable silence. His hand finds my ankle, and he rubs his thumb back and forth over the bony protrusion. I can't tell what he's looking at. All I know is that I'm looking at *him*.

"You know," he starts, after maybe three minutes or a half hour has gone by in lazy perfection, "I forgot one important part the other day when I submitted my information to the Kinsley Board."

I'm already laughing, because he knows how to thread a joke throughout eternity as well as I do. "Oooh, I don't know how they're going to handle a late submission. They insist on punctuality."

"Maybe I can sway them." The corners of his lips curl up, and I almost ask him to raise his sunglasses so I can see how intensely he's watching me right now. "Your toes."

"My toes have turned you on?"

He nods, squeezing each of my feet in turn. "Oh, yeah."

"I don't understand how that's possible."

"It's okay. We can chalk it up to a medical mystery, if that helps."

I dissolve into laughter again. "I don't think that helps, actually. I'd rather not be featured on some TLC reality show because of a man's interest in my toes."

He grabs my other ankle and gives me a little tug. "You know what? Get over here."

It's hard not to comply with any little thing he wants. I scoot his way, and he adjusts himself on the big bench seat so that we're cuddling, our legs intertwined even though it's hot and sticky out.

"I've got another medical mystery for you to check out," he murmurs into my ear, which prompts more laughter on my end.

"Does it have something to do with this protrusion between your legs?"

"Mm-hmm." He rolls onto his back, guiding me on top of him. I land on his cock, which is already mostly hard. Maybe my pink toes *do* work wonders. It's impossible to imagine—*my toes?*—but hey, the science is here. I'm not one to dispute data.

"Mmmm." My eyes flutter shut as I ease my legs open wide, settling down on top of him in *just* the right spot. I prop my palms on the vinyl cushion on either side of him, rocking my hips back and forth.

The clothing barrier is low between us, which means this might get out of control fast. He's in charcoal-gray swim trunks, and I've got my pink-and-white striped bathing suit. His hands scorch up the sides of my waist, and then he pushes off the bikini cups so that my breasts spill free.

"Easy, there!" I glance around. The other boaters might not appreciate our display of nudity.

"Nobody is looking," he assures me. And he's right. The nearest boat is probably a half mile away. The Sand Bar is blessedly unpopulated today, and the others would have to be watching us with binoculars to get a sense of what we were doing over here, half-protected by the railing of the bow. "Nobody except me," he adds, which sends a hot shiver up my spine.

Our lips collide then, sticky and passionate and rough. We make out so hard that he's grunting and I'm groaning, unattractive noises that only stoke the fire further. He's got my ass cheeks in both hands again, fingertips digging into that sensitive flesh right near the start of my pussy. I'm already aching for him, drenched and ready, my nipples so hard that they might break through my bikini.

Once we pull apart, breathless and wild-eyed, Connor grabs my face between his hands. "Why are you magic?"

I smile. He's exaggerating. It's the pheromones speaking.

"Why are you perfect?" I ask, pushing my hands across the warm expanse of his pecs, down the ridges of his abs. I am *not* exaggerating. This man is perfection embodied.

He wets his bottom lip. "Kins. I wanna be in you."

I dip down for another kiss. "Where'd you put the condoms?"

"In my backpack."

I crawl off him and reach for the bag he stowed in the corner. I resume my perch, pussy covering cock, and start to paw through his bag. I find the condom box as promised—we got the mega stash last week—but when I go rummaging inside, I don't see a single condom.

"Connor..."

"What?"

I double and triple check, then I show the bag to him. "We're out."

His mouth parts, and he gives the bag a once over, too. Then he deflates back onto the cushion. "Fuck. Have we had that much sex?"

"My hips have been sore for a full week. So...yeah."

He laughs, smoothing his palms over the tops of my thighs. He shifts beneath me, which pushes the tip of his cock right against my clit. My head drops back, and a low moan escapes me. God, I still want him. Without the condom.

I've never done it that way with anyone except my ex. Connor is already a thousand times more deserving of something so intimate than my ex ever was.

"Do we have to..." I cock my head. "You know..."

He wets his bottom lip again. "You want to?"

"I'm on birth control. And I trust you."

He grunts, his abs flexing as he pushes his hips against me again. "Where do you want me to come?"

I gulp. "Inside me."

"Oh my God. I'm gonna lose my mind." He blows out a long breath. Then he props up on his elbows. "Take your swimsuit off, babe."

His voice is softer now. I'm not entirely sure what this change is that I'm seeing, but I get it. This feels like a big step. At least, it is for me. But I wouldn't suggest this with him unless I really trusted him. Unless I...loved him? It sounds absurd to even think about, but it's true. I've known Connor peripherally my whole life, and these two weeks have only cemented what my teenaged self always suspected about him.

Connor is still my dream man, and I want to share this inexplicably intimate act with him.

I step onto wobbly legs and slide my bikini bottoms down. He shimmies out of his swim trunks, his cock springing free. The familiar sight of tightly trimmed hair framing his massive centerpiece makes my core clench. He reaches for me then, urging me back on top of him.

I slide onto him with reverent slowness. He undoes the strings of my top and slides it off. We're both buck naked in the middle of Briggs Bay, and I couldn't care less. I'm 99 percent horny and 1 percent thankful I applied sunscreen.

The breeze whips around me as I prop my palms against his abs, sliding my slick pussy back and forth over his cock. The heat between our legs is fiercer than the mid-day sun. Our skin sticks where my thighs meet his.

But none of this bothers me. In fact, it only heightens the anticipation. The heat of the day bearing down on us has forced me into some type of dreamworld, where Connor and I are the only two who matter and this thing between us is undeniable. Inescapable. It's hard to imagine the rest of my life without being able to tap into this invigorating, sexy connection we've cultivated over the past week and a half. The rest of my life won't be nearly as interesting if Connor isn't part of it.

The thought thuds through me, but I distract myself from it by pushing my hips up and positioning myself on the tip of Connor's dick. Sex is an *excellent* distraction. The fiery heat of him pushes into me, my entrance wet and waiting for him.

And then I slide down, down, down, engulfing him, easing onto him so slowly that I don't know whether I want to cry or scream. Without a condom, it's different. It's so much better than great. It's fucking outstanding, with nothing separating the flesh of us, him buried to the hilt inside me. Tears prick my eyes—yet another thing I choose to ignore. I pinch my eyes shut, head tipping back.

"Fuuuuuuuuuck." His voice comes out gravelly, deeper than I've ever heard it.

I swing my head in a slow circle. I have no voice. I have no thoughts. I am only *lovemaking.*

He thrusts his hips beneath me, finding an extra millimeter inside me. I cry out, scraping my nails against his chest. When I open my eyes, he's tugging my arms.

"Come here, come here." He urges me to lie down on top of him. His big arms go tight around me, and I'm in a hot cocoon of sensuality and perfection and the most beguiling heartbeat I've ever heard thrumming in another human's chest. I melt against him, sweatiness be damned. He moves his hips in a slow, rhythmic circle. My breath escapes me in labored pants.

We're barely moving, yet somehow this is the most erotic, most sensual sex I've had in my life.

He nuzzles my neck, lips sliding against the sweaty skin there. Then his mouth finds mine, salty sweet and copper, and we kiss so hard and deeply that I almost come from the make-out session alone. Doing anything while he's buried inside me—filling me like this, throbbing and tense—is grounds for coming. He could give a PowerPoint presentation while his dick was inside me, and it might push me over the edge.

"Connor," I finally whisper, my voice sticking in my throat. "It feels too good."

He snags my lips in another kiss, and then he rolls us over, depositing me back-down on the bench. He coaxes my knees up to his sides, and he groans when he finds even more depth inside me.

"Kinsley," he pants, teeth grazing my ear lobe. A shiver races through me, and I arch up, needing more of him. "You're a sunbeam, you know that?"

His comment makes me smile. He's pushing himself in and out, faster now, his slick chest slipping against my tits. Every inch of us is sweating and erotic and sexier than sin. I think I've been orgasming the entire time without realizing it.

"That's sweet," I murmur, my hands trailing over the rippling muscles of his back as he fucks me. As he makes love to me. I'm not sure which it is anymore, because this is different from anything I've ever experienced before. It's deeper. It's more meaningful. It's so raw that I want to cry, and I don't even know why.

He pushes himself inside me again. He huffs. "You're Sunny-kins."

His cock fills me one last time, and something in the combination of the water lapping nearby combined with the explosive heat of him, inside and on top of me, finally shoves me over the edge. My legs go rigid, and I toss my head back, a brutally fast orgasm tearing through me. A pinched cry escapes me as the heat and bliss and wonder all assault me in equal measure.

Connor is groaning now too, hips jerking. And then I feel it, the liquid heat of him filling me, coating my insides and dribbling out between my legs. We hold each other for a long time, sighing and panting and groaning. Trying to recover from this tidal wave of emotion and pleasure that submerged us.

When he finally slips out of me, the pond between my legs is noticeable. I prop myself up on my elbows, looking down in disbelief. He hobbles off and returns a moment later with a rag to wipe it up, starting with me.

His cheeks are red, skin still glistening from our slip-n-slide sex, as he gently cleans me up. Then he wipes down the cushion. Tosses the rag.

And then he gets on his knees beside the bench and gives me a kiss so deep and meaningful that I have no choice but to believe.

This thing between us?

It's real as fuck.

# CHAPTER TWENTY-ONE

CONNOR

Two days left until our flight back to San Diego, and we're hitting up the Daily Shop in a textbook definition of a liquor run.

Kinsley and I are straight lovebirds. We go from mid-aisle smooching to running toward the chip display like kids, to shouting from one end of the aisle to the other when she finds the exact brand of rum she was looking for.

With Kinsley, everything is more fun. Absolutely everything.

I didn't even know that I could feel this way about someone. God knows most outings with Tamara were more chore than childlike. Honestly, the way Kinsley and I are together feels more like a movie than real life.

"Over here." She steers me by squeezing my waist. I bury my nose in the top of her head, inhaling the sweet scent of her shampoo. We round a corner, and then she gasps.

Like, holy-shit-I-almost-stepped-in-front-of-a-car gasps.

A man and a woman stare back at us, blinking dully.

"Mom and Dad?" Kinsley squeaks.

My gaze bounces between the two of them. Yes, Kinsley does oddly resemble both of them. She takes more after her dad, though, with the long, straight nose and, well, those ears.

Those ears which are pretty adorable, actually.

"Kinsley!" Her mom's eyebrows rocket to the top of her head, a grimace-smile covering her face.

"What are you two doing here?" Kinsley asks. Then she sighs. "I mean...I thought...I wasn't expecting..."

Her parents' gazes swing my way. Suddenly, there are a lot of questions clogging up the silence.

"This is Connor Daly," Kinsley says.

"We know who he is," her dad affirms.

"We, uh..." Kinsley looks up at me. I can read the *oh shit* clearly in her eyes. "We've been, you know. Dating."

I offer a smile. I have no idea what to do here. This might actually be worse than my own parents. They are staring military-grade daggers my way, and I'm fairly certain one of them is going to physically remove my arm from around Kinsley's shoulders.

Mr. and Mrs. Cabana straighten. Her dad clears his throat.

"Are you still coming over for dinner and euchre tonight?" Her mom asks in a clipped tone. Suspiciously like the one my mom uses with Kinsley.

"Yeah." She looks up at me again. "Is that okay, Connor?"

"Of course." I try to look friendly. Affable. Just a regular old son-of-your-nemesis.

Kinsley looks at her parents then, nibbling on her lip. "Can Connor come too?"

Mr. and Mrs. exchange unreadable looks, and then her mom shrugs. "Sure."

Kinsley squeezes my hand that is dangling over her shoulder. "Okay. I'll bring wine."

"RumChata," I tease, knocking her with my hip.

Her mom's eyes narrow to slits, so I vow to remain silent until this is over.

"See you at six," her dad says, and they both walk stiffly past us. Kinsley watches them go, and then she collapses into my side.

"Okay, I was wrong," she moans into my shoulder. "They're all bad."

"We are definitely the adults now," I agree. We resume a lazy pace down the bread aisle. My mind flashes to what she told them—*we're dating*. Which, we are. Technically. But also not. Because we've erased all the lines of what makes sense. On the one hand, I'm falling for her, and hard. On the other hand, I'm not looking for a relationship and this is just fun.

But how do we even start that conversation?

It's easier to ignore it, honestly.

We pay for our things and head back to my parents' house, where we change into nicer clothes. She wears flowy black and gold striped pants with a black crop top. Paired with her long, blonde braid, she's stunning. I can't rip my gaze off her while she's pushing hoop earrings in at the mirror.

"What?" she asks. "Thinking about that pizza place again?"

I smirk. "Yes. Because you've known all along pizza was code for your ass."

"At least you don't call me pizza ass."

I squeeze one of her perfect butt cheeks, sucking on my bottom lip as my cock twitches to life. "Do we have to go to your parents' house?"

"I do, at least." She sighs, turning to face me. "You aren't obligated, though."

"No." I press a soft kiss to her lips. "I'll go. I want to."

I drive the rental car to the farthest eastern reaches of Bayshore, where her family lives in a ritzy sub-division with stone-paved driveways and lots of big, bushy trees. There are lots of rich boaters in this part of the world, what with Lake Erie being the perfect attraction. Her mom opens the door, wearing her nautical blue ballcap over her low, platinum-blonde ponytail. She's wearing a tank top that says *Lake Mode* and tan Sperry's. All in all, she is the quintessential casual summer boater.

And Kinsley's parents' house is *nice*. It's an expanded cottage with a loft and a fully finished basement that her parents have turned into a party space. The table is already set and waiting for us, big bay windows overlooking the sloping backyard lined with bushes and the occasional rose bush. A tub full of beer sits on ice on the kitchen island.

Now I'm on the receiving end of the avoidance. Her dad offers me one beer, and after that, her parents don't say much to me. They are tolerating me, at best. And while I sit back and absorb their conversation—talking about Kestrel's job in Columbus and Katie's internship and what Kinsley plans to do with the warranty of the used car she bought—I realize that the man and woman in front of me used to be *best friends* with my own parents.

And now?

They'll hardly acknowledge the offspring of the other.

How sad. But I know it's not for nothing. I've never gotten a straight story out of my mom, and God knows my dad would never tell me specifics. Sometimes, it seems like the story will never come out. I just wonder: in a different world, would Kinsley and I have grown up as best friends? Maybe even lovers?

Dinner churns by, uneventful and yummy. We have rib eyes and mashed potatoes, with plenty of beer. When it comes time for euchre, the ubiquitous Midwestern card game, Kinsley and I are partners against her parents. After a few rounds, some of the tension melts away. By round four, my unexpected loner hand has the whole table shouting. Kinsley and I end up losing, but only by one point.

Once the card game wraps up and Kinsley says that it's time for us to head back to my house, her parents tighten up all over again. All the goodwill: evaporated.

Her mom makes a point of keeping Kinsley back, speaking to her in low tones. I linger by the huge front door, trying not to look like I'm eavesdropping while doing exactly that. When Kinsley comes into the hallway, she's frowning, and she leads us out of the house without another word.

Dusk has crept over the world by now, the last rays of the sunset we missed finally sinking away from the world. Crickets chirp from indeterminate spots in the heavily mulched landscaping lining her parents' house. Once we're inside the car, she tugs down the mirror in her visor and looks at her teeth.

"What was that about?" I start the car and slowly reverse down the driveway.

"Oh, just a reminder that I'm acting out due to being the middle child." She scoffs, then slams the visor shut.

I smirk. "That sounds familiar."

"They don't understand why I had to go all the way to the West Coast when Katie and Kestrel are perfectly fine here in Ohio. And they don't understand why…" She gestures to the space between us. "Of all the people in the world…"

*Well, good thing this isn't real, then.* The words dance in the back of my throat, but they don't make the leap past my lips.

I'm not entirely sure that it's true. And it might not even help if it were.

"We need to figure out what happened between the four of them." I ease the car forward and begin the long drive out of the neighborhood.

"Yeah." She crosses her arms, staring out the window. "I plan to figure that out ASAP."

# CHAPTER TWENTY-TWO



Our last full day and night in Bayshore blurs by in an exciting rush. We visit the beach again, have one last ping-pong battle, and Connor takes me to Grayson's house to see all the renovations they've managed to accomplish in so little time.

And then before I know it, it's nine p.m. and we're walking to the beach at the end of the street for the second time that day, and the last time of our trip. A bonfire snags our attention, so we head there. And what do you know—Grayson is there, with Hazel in his lap. The two of them are way cuter than I can even handle. We join the group of old Bayshore High friends. Someone brings a guitar, and music accompanies our beer drinking and laughter.

It's idyllic, not to mention the perfect ending to what is most definitely my favorite visit back home since the dawn of time. Leaving work drama and life quandaries behind for two weeks? I've never needed this more. Cultivating a satisfying relationship with my long-time heartthrob? Holy shit, the icing on this cake reaches a mile high.

Connor and I neck on a blanket for a little while, then he goes to play nighttime beach volleyball with Gray. I head for the empty seat at Hazel's side. She smiles at me as I sit beside her.

"Hey there," I say.

"Kinsley." She squeezes my arm. "Or should I say Mrs. Connor Daly?"

I laugh. Her comment satisfies me all the way down to my bone marrow. "Aren't you Mrs. Grayson Daly?"

"Definitely not," she says with a laugh. "I mean...I don't know. Maybe someday. Somehow."

We both watch the crackling fire for a moment. Most of the friends have drifted toward the volleyball, so we can speak in relative privacy. I nibble on my lip as I turn over a thought in my head.

"Connor and I really aren't...*that* serious," I say, unsure how to explain the dynamic at work here. "But I want us to be that serious. I just..." I rub at my face. I didn't realize asking her for help would be so embarrassing. "I kind of want to...surprise him."

"In what way?"

I watch the flames licking at the domed steel grating encasing the bonfire pit. "Like...with how I dress. And how I do my makeup." I swing my gaze over to her. She's dressed down today, wearing an OSU sweatshirt and cotton shorts, but she's got the fierce eyebrows and perfect lashes of a total babe. I want her face. I want her style. And I need her as my mentor. "I thought maybe you could help me."

"Kinsley, you don't need help," she starts.

"No. I do. You haven't seen even a third of my wardrobe. It's pretty bad."

She tuts. "You're a natural beauty. You don't need makeup."

"Well, that's what I think about you, but you still wear it."

Hazel tips her head to one side. "Fine. What are you thinking about doing?"

I shrug, letting a puff of air escape. "There's this quarter-end party at work that is always super fun and elegant. I'd like to look *really good* there. Because I'll be going with Connor, and..." I falter, because I realize that we haven't even talked about any of this. The impressing. The dressing. The *dating*. But I know it's going to happen.

Because for once, I'm confident about what's happening between us.

We haven't talked about it yet, but I know.

And I know *he knows*.

"Ooh. You should come to the Bicentennial Ball instead," Hazel says.

"I wish. That would probably be way more fun than this summer party E-bid always has." I pause. "Though they do have *quite* excellent tiny cakes."

"That does sound nice," Hazel agrees.

"Except it's all work colleagues, and, let's be real, not all of them are great." I'm thinking specifically of my boss. She's the main part of it that I dread each year, and maybe coming dolled up will help me tolerate her more. Especially if I have Connor on my arm.

"I definitely think I can help make this year's party better than ever," Hazel says with a genuine smile. There's practically a twinkle in her eye—though it might be the reflection of the fire—and I know why 90 percent of the county chooses her as their realtor. I'm not even mad about it. My dad is the other main realtor in town. He has his own faithful clients...and Hazel has the rest.

We chat a little while longer, until Connor and Grayson race past us, kicking up sand and shouting about a fluke. Grayson tackles Connor further down the beach, while Maverick cracks up and some of Grayson's buddies egg it all on. Connor comes up laughing a moment later, and then Maverick shoves Grayson. The whole cycle starts again.

I don't know what they're fake fighting about, but seeing it makes my heart warm. I want to be part of this family. I can tolerate Annette and Damon never truly talking to me. Hell, maybe that's for the better. They won't interfere in our life choices and insert themselves in our parenting approach when we finally decide to raise kids or puppies or neither. Christmas might be awkward, but there should be less drama overall if we never truly speak to one another.

Some couples probably wish for this arrangement! We're so lucky to have it right off the bat.

My phone vibrates, yanking me out of my rationalization.

*MOM: Let me give you one last hug! We're down at the marina. Just want to see my Kinsie. Alone.*

I roll my eyes, not that she can see it. What a subtle way to say *No Dalys Allowed.* They dock right outside High-5's, which is a quick walk from here. I tell Hazel I'm going to go say bye to my parents real quick, then I scout out Connor, who has his knee in Maverick's back and has him pinned into the sand.

"Connor?" I dodge a spray of sand as Maverick fights to free himself.

"Babe, we're establishing the hierarchy," he says through laughter.

"Okay, well, I'm gonna go to High-5's real quick. I'll be back super-fast."

"All right, hurry back," he says, then doubles down on Maverick. "You don't want to miss my victory." As his brother howls, I take my chance to leave quietly.

The night is unseasonably cool. I take in deep breaths of the fresh lake air, because I need to store it away, or bury it deeper into my cells. The boardwalk is softly lit by round little lights set into the wooden walkway. I pass strolling couples and the occasional single gal or guy, just taking it all in.

I'm sad to leave Bayshore. I don't know when I might be back, and furthermore, if any visit home will ever be as epic as this one.

But more than that, this visit home has been a gift. One that I'm still not entirely sure how to utilize.

My feet thud down the wooden docks as I hurry to my parents' slip. Mom's trademark ballcap with the name of their marina is on her head, her blonde ponytail swinging as she raises a beer to greet me. Since we kids flew the coop, my mom and dad turned into the partiers they've always dreamt of being. It's funny seeing them flourish in their fifties. They go harder than I do at age twenty-five. It's a work night, for God's sake.

"Kinsieee," my mom says, wrapping me in a big hug. She's not toasted, but she's getting there. I know her drunken stages, and this is about a two out of five.

"I'm going to miss you two," I say. And it's true. There's nothing like being back in the warm embrace of home, where every item in my parent's house is curated and comfortable and too expensive for my budget out west.

"When do you fly out, honey?" Dad asks, sinking into the vinyl equivalent of a La-z-Boy at the back of the boat. Cards are splayed out on a folding table near the back bench. Tiny palm-tree lights are strung along the top rails of their dock, and the neighbors on the slip to the right are laughing loudly about something. This is their happy place. Surrounded by friends and water and boats.

It makes me wonder. Where's my happy place?

"Tomorrow at noon," I say. Bayshore is a happy place, but it's not *the* happy place. And even though I've had an amazing two weeks here, I'm ready to get back to the ocean bustle of San Diego.

"Did you have a good trip?" Mom's tone holds a note of caution. They probably realize that I wasn't visiting a friend all along, but they don't need to know all the details about my life. I can tell them what I choose to.

"Yes. We had an amazing time." Ah, the cryptic *we*. Mom clears her throat. Definitely not going to tell her that I spread my sex juices all over the bow the other day. Even though I thoroughly sanitized once Connor and I made it back to the dock.

"Listen. I want to tell you something"—she reaches for my wrist, giving it a motherly squeeze—"from one woman to another."

I nod, waiting for her to go on.

"The Daly family." She rolls her lips inward, shaking her head as she inspects something on the ground. "They are *not* to be trusted. I thought I had made this very clear when you were younger."

"Yeah, you did."

"He will *use you*," mom insists. "Because that family is full of users and abusers."

I can't help but roll my eyes. But in the back of my mind, something pings. The whole start of this trip was a type of using me, wasn't it? Connor wanted to use me to play his girlfriend.

But no. It wasn't using me if I agreed to it. That was then. And this is now. We've gone way past the ruse into *reality*.

"You don't believe me," she says, wagging her finger at me. "You don't, but I swear to you. Please be careful with him. I don't like that you're with him—"

"Lisa," my dad starts.

"—but you need to be made aware." She slices her hands through the air.

I nibble on my lip, shifting from one foot to the other. "Okay, and what do you have to say about it, dad?"

He sighs, reaching for his beer. "I feel the same as your mother."

"What even happened? And why does it still matter all these years later?"

My mom watches me for a few moments, nibbling on her lip in exactly the same way that I do. "Annette and I used to be best friends.

The very best friends you could have hoped for. But she did not take kindly to the fact that I fell in love with your father."

I blink, looking between Mom and Dad. "So she was…"

"She was with your father first," Mom whispers, "but they weren't compatible, and it ended. I waited until the appropriate time before I ever said how I felt."

"Once she got pregnant with the first one"—Dad can only mean Dominic—"she called and tried to say it was mine."

"She only wanted money," Mom spits. "Because that horse of a husband of hers was broke."

My mind is spinning with these long-gone details. Damon Daly, broke? I can't even imagine it.

"One look at that boy, and it was clear he wasn't mine." Dad huffs, looking as shocked as if it had happened last week. "Besides, it was physically impossible. We hadn't been together in so long."

I blink, looking between the two of them, trying to imagine my dad with Annette. The idea refuses to fit together. What if Dad had stayed with Annette? *Could I have almost been born a Daly?*

Mom looks back at Dad, and something unknowable to me shivers between them. She reaches out for his hand and squeezes it. I rub at my forehead, suddenly exhausted by all of this.

This is their drama. Not mine. And it has nothing to do with Connor and me.

"I hear what you're saying. I'll tread carefully." Though by *carefully*, I think I really mean *run headfirst toward Connor with open arms*.

"There are so many other things they've done over the years," Mom goes on, flicking her wrist. "The laundry list would bore you as much as it would scandalize."

Mom sends me off with about a hundred kisses, and Dad squeezes me long and hard and tells me to kick ass out west like I've been doing. I get a lump in my throat and nod. I don't know how much ass kicking I've really been doing. More like ass wiping.

Because at the end of the day, I'm just Tamara's bitch, and she knows that I know it. I scuff back toward the beach, glummer than at the start of my vacation. Two weeks ago, I had all this time off to look forward to. Now? I'm faced with the reality of returning to work with the woman who sparks a knot in my stomach every freaking morning.

Connor's words return to me while I'm scuffing my way back down the boardwalk.

*Let's work on the eye contact thing.*

He'd said it so good-naturedly, so matter-of-factly. Like it was equal parts regular thought, casual suggestion, and challenge.

I should take a page from Connor's book.

Let's work on the shitty job thing. I'm tired of dreading my work life, of not knowing what to do next.

When I get back to San Diego, I'm going to give E-bid one last shot to make it the dream job I know it can be.

# CHAPTER TWENTY-THREE

CONNOR

It doesn't sink in that we've left Bayshore until we're buckling our seat belts in business class on our return flight.

How have two weeks gone by already? I look over at Kinsley, who is smoothing down her billowy black pants before she settles into a paperback. I have to fight to keep the grin off my face.

We started as strangers, but we might as well be long-term spouses at this point. I feel like I know her inside and out...but yet, with so much more to discover still. With two fully sexy and idyllic weeks under our belts, I know one thing for certain: I want to continue the good times.

But as the plane taxis and we lift off, my thoughts turn toward San Diego.

I sent Tamara my finished app earlier this week in a last-ditch effort to extract whatever ounce of goodwill she might still feel about me. Because even though we're toxic together, she might still want to see me succeed.

But I've gotten zero response so far, and I'm not hopeful. Which means that as soon as I'm back to the daily grind, I'm starting the hunt for a new job. My number one priority is getting my career in order, no matter what.

What does that mean for Kinsley and me? I didn't want anything serious before this. Hell, I didn't want *anything*. But now I have this ready-made girlfriend, and it feels a little bit too easy to contemplate continuing things how we've been doing them.

And if I'm honest with myself? I want to keep this up. Even though I wasn't planning on this, there's something so soft and sensual about Kinsley. We laugh our asses off together. We have fun wherever we go, whatever we do. She's beautiful and weird and smart.

She's my dream woman.

The one I definitely wasn't looking for.

Kinsley rests her head on my shoulder as she reads, as though she can sense the vortex of thoughts inside my skull pertaining directly to her. I brush my lips against the top of my head, and she stops reading to smile up at me. Then she buries herself in her book again.

Yeah. I don't want this to end. But I'm not sure how to move forward.

We should talk about it. That much is clear. But as the flight whiles on, I turn on my in-seat TV screen and find a new series to watch. *The Handmaid's Tale*. It's way more intense than I bargained for. A little while later, Kinsley abandons her book and watches my screen for a little bit. I offer her one of my ear buds. We settle in to watch, alternating between gasps and the occasional shout.

Our screens have to physically turn off during landing before we break for air. Kinsley and I share wide eyes as we land. I grab her hand and don't let go until it's time to get off the plane.

The walk through the airport passes like a dream. We're floating—caught between vacation and the start of work; between our regular lives here in San Diego and the fantasy bubble we created in Bayshore. It's hard to know what to do. How to act. Whether or not to invite her back to my apartment.

I use the restroom while she's waiting for the bags, trying to imagine what spending the night without her will feel like. Spoiler alert: the outlook is grim. I need to figure out a way to get her back to my place, or vice versa, without looking like a needy asshole. When I come out, she's tugged both our bags off the conveyor belt.

She's fiddling with the tip of her braid when I approach. She rolls my bag toward me. "Here. I got this for you."

"Thanks."

She laughs a little, her gaze falling to her own olive drab bag. Silence stretches between us.

"Do you—" she begins.

"What are you—" I say at exactly the same time.

We both laugh. I grip the handle of my bag as if I need it for balance.

"You go first," I tell her.

She nibbles on her lip. "I was going to ask if you want to keep watching the series at my house."

Relief floods me. Yes. *Yes.* This is the perfect excuse, and man, I need it. I don't know why this is so hard, but it is. This was supposed to be the end of whatever we had going, but we can extend it for one more night. Because it makes sense. Because we want to.

Because I've already grown so attached to Kinsley that I'm not sure I can fathom a night away from her.

We call a ride share, and the trip to her apartment is quick. We bust inside, pure laughter and smooches, confronting the musty air and the trash she forgot to take out. I offer to take out the offending bag while she unpacks a little and showers. When I come back in, the water is running, a dull rush from deep inside the bedroom. Her place is quirky and comfy, just like her. I check out the pictures on the wall—mostly family, a few weird shots of sunflowers and abandoned washing machines—and then head into her bedroom.

But when I look out at the cityscape of San Diego stretching away from her tenth-floor window, I remember that I have my own life here. My own routines. We can't keep living like we did in Bayshore. It won't fit here.

So it's important to me that I get a feel for what it might be like to *not* have this connection. What life would be like if I *couldn't* waltz into her bedroom and get naked and surprise her in the shower. Is it even possible anymore?

I linger near the bed, checking out the scant progress she's made on her luggage. I clench and unclench my teeth, counseling myself to go back to seeing her the way I did before. Shapeless. Uninteresting. Non-provocative.

But she's in the shower right now, and God, I know how much she likes shower sex. I roll my neck in a slow circle. And then I start counting down slowly from ten.

I don't make it to eight before I'm shucking my pants and tearing off my T-shirt. This is the proof I need. Kinsley's got me wrapped around her finger, and I have no idea what comes next.

Except this. I ease into the bathroom, which is already clogged with steam and the floral scent of her shampoo. I quietly slide open the shower door and step into the stall. When she opens her eyes from rinsing out her hair, she screams.

"Connor!"

"Correct. You win the prize." My grin is a mile wide, and I grip her slippery hips, bringing our bodies flush together. A throaty laugh escapes her.

"What's the prize?"

"Everything you see here." I kiss her smiling lips, over and over again, coaxing needy kisses from her. She wraps her arms around my neck, and before I can think twice, I've hoisted her, bringing her body crashing against the vinyl wall of the shower. Warm water rushes over my back, and we don't break the kiss for anything. Our teeth crash, tongues pushing, as I wiggle my hips between her legs.

Her thighs spread, a silky yield that feels like coming home. I've been shacking up with her for almost two full weeks, but somehow it feels like years. Our mouths are hungry, seeking, urgent against each other while I flex my hips and then find that sweet, damp core of her that is always ready and waiting for me.

She moans through a kiss while I plunge inside her, her silky stretch the only thing I can see and feel and think about. Now, and probably forever. My shoulders prickle as I work myself in and out of her, our kisses stalling and then starting, feverish and then lethargic.

Kinsley claws at my back, arching herself into me, inviting me even deeper. As though I could possibly be buried any more inside this woman. I hoist her again, her ass like melons in my hands, and she cries out, sharp and loud in the humid air. She goes weak and wilted in my arms, collapsing against me, her lips finally sliding away from mine.

She finds the hollow of my neck, whispering my name over and over. I thrust into her again and let the glorious rush of pleasure pummel through me and into her, filling her to overflowing. My thighs tense as the orgasm threatens to topple me, but I hold her as tightly as I can, bracing myself against the storm.

When the clouds clear, her eyes are hooded and she looks as wrung out as a towel. It was one of our shorter sessions, but definitely one of the most intense. I smooth my lips over her cheek, across the bridge of her nose. I've had all of her and more, but I can't keep myself away.

Kinsley's eyes flutter, and then I'm staring into the periwinkle galaxy of her gaze. The water rushes down around us while we just watch. Staring, searching for something that words don't define and nobody else can understand.

It feels like hours until I finally set her down onto her own two feet. I finish soaping her up, and then she does the same for me. It's still early when we towel off, but without a word we both ease into bed. My bags remain untouched; her half-unpacked duffel gets shoved to the floor.

Something has changed between us tonight. And as she settles into my arms to fall asleep, I finally realize what it means for me.

My life won't feel right without her.

That much, I know for certain.

But I'm not sure I'm ready for her, dream woman or not.

# CHAPTER TWENTY-FOUR

KINSLEY

The *beep, beep, beep* of my alarm is the first thing I'm aware of on Monday morning. A stretch overtakes me, followed by a grin that only Connor is responsible for.

My body is sore—again—but it's a minor inconvenience for the brand of physical and emotional pleasure I've been enjoying. I'll gladly hobble around if it means Connor keeps making love to me like he did last night in the shower.

I yawn, rolling onto my side, flinging an arm out in search of Connor.

But my hand flops against cool sheets, not the welcoming, warm curve of a heaven-formed bicep. There is nobody beside me in bed. I sit up, as alert as if I'd started my morning coffee. I rub my eyes as I adjust to the dim surroundings. It's six a.m., and the tawny hue of dawn is already creeping around the edges of my blinds.

I listen to the apartment. For the telltale sounds of footsteps in the kitchen or the rush of a morning pee.

Connor isn't here.

And his bags are gone too.

I frown and ease out of bed, more disconcerted than I'd like by the absence. He probably said goodbye to me while I was asleep. That's all. He probably gave me a kiss and left a note on my kitchen counter.

But when I shuffle into my quiet and still-sorta-gross-smelling kitchen, there's no note.

In fact, there's no sign that Connor was ever here. That he ever existed.

Panic streaks through me as I entertain the wild notion that the whole thing was a dream. Two weeks spent in some sort of psychosis. Like in *Inception*, when he's under for two hours but he's lived an entire life in his dream space. That's me. I've incepted Connor and all that shower sex, when really I've been fast asleep in San Diego, and it's still two Fridays ago.

Adrenaline streaks through me as anxiety takes root.

It can't possibly be true.

But oh, how the monkey mind loves to entertain the possibility of it.

I go through the motions of my morning routine. Cold shower, start the coffee pot, rummage for clothes, try on three things, hate them all, swear while I realize the coffee maker's been beeping for ten minutes, check my phone. I'm almost late.

I've chosen the same old, same old work outfit. Flared taupe pants, a ruffled brown and white polka-dotted blouse. I've swept my tresses back into the same old, same old braid.

And I head out the door to my same old, same old job.

But today, I've got a volcano rumbling to life in me. I don't feel the same old Kinsley on the inside. There's something different afoot. Something potentially explosive, with lava flows and probably magma, if we're getting technical. Definitely anxiety, since I'm still not sure if Bayshore was a fever dream.

Before I head inside for the day, I send Connor a message.
*KINSLEY: I miss you already.*

I breeze into E-bid right on time at 7:55 a.m. My stomach turns to prickles and tension as I wait for any hint of Connor. Waiting for that first glance. The first smirk. The first time he'll lean over my shoulder while I'm seated at my desk and whisper something into the shell of my ear.

*Yes.* I can't wait to be on the receiving end of his private looks and sexy winks. Or even a mouthed 'sea gull' from across the lunchroom.

I'm in before Tamara—typical—and I settle in at my desk to get caught up on work email. I'll probably be doing this most of the morning, until Tamara comes up with some surprise bitch task to make my life miserable.

I'm checking my phone every three minutes, peering into the top drawer of my desk to see if Connor has written back. Nothing. But it's fine, because he's busy, and he's probably getting caught up like I am. More than likely he's in a meeting, just *waiting* to text me back. He's probably got the emojis lined up and waiting for him to press Send.

Tamara's heels clack across the floor of the HR wing around nine a.m. She's got folders in her arms, her dark brown hair pulled back into a low, fierce bun. Her lips look bigger today. Maybe she outlined them with extra thick pencil or got those weird injections to "inflate your pout." That makes me think of puffer fishes, though, which forces me to bite back a laugh.

Tamara's emerald green gaze snaps my way. She doesn't say hi. She doesn't ask how my vacation was. Voice like a switchblade, she says, "Kinsley, come with me."

I push to standing, my stomach shrinking to an acorn. I follow in her irritated trail, which smells like freesia and condescension, and once we get inside her office she barks, "Close the door."

I do as she says and sink into the chair facing her desk. She doesn't look at me as she organizes files and puts order to an otherwise-immaculate desk. I rub my palms back and forth over the knees of my pants, trying to *feel* friendly toward her.

"So, what's this about?" I finally venture, once the silence has become deafening.

"You have put me *really behind*," she says, a frown tugging her inflated pout downward. "So behind that the controller has gotten involved."

Great. Here we go. Why I'm the reason everything is wrong.

"Your performance report was due at the start of your 'personal days.'" She uses air quotes. "And since you didn't think to ask whether or not you'd be abandoning outstanding duties or throwing your higher-ups under the bus," she gestures around her, "here we are."

I blink, not quite sure how to process this. All of my grievances with Tamara can be distilled into this moment. No matter what I do, there is something I've done *exceptionally wrong* that I must atone for.

"I'm sorry," I mutter.

"Yeah. I'm sure you are." The condescension drips from her words as she turns toward her laptop and clicks through some screens. A disgusted silence settles between us, and as I'm about to try to lighten the mood or otherwise cajole her, I feel the volcano rumble to life again. Lava's pushing through my veins. I hear Connor's voice. *Let's work on the eye contact thing.*

So I look Tamara straight in the face. And I stare at her.

My taking personal days on a whim isn't the reason she's behind. This performance report is not the reason for her bad mood. *She* is the reason for all those things. And I'm half tempted to shout this at her before finding a book I can rip in two and then run off into the sunset like a snarling wolf, seeking another victim.

I don't do the wolf stuff. Instead, I stare more. I don't make the mood lighter or nicer.

Because she also made this unsavory stew, and she can sit in it too.

When she looks over at me, I swear I see surprise flash across her face. Like she wasn't expecting my serial killer-grade stare.

"Let's begin?" She clears her throat and launches into the most boring rendition of corporate speak I could ever hope to suffer through. She outlines each of my duties and the ways in which I'm barely accomplishing them. From what she's saying, it's a wonder I even have a job. And to be honest, I can barely listen to the scathing account of my underperformance, partly because I'm wracking my brain to figure out how I'm falling so short of the low bar that's set for me here.

It doesn't make sense. I try my hardest, and it's the opposite of enough.

A phone call interrupts us, and Tamara takes it. She murmurs, "Mmhmm," into the phone over and over again. When she hangs up, she sighs.

"I need to pause this. Something's come up."

I make sure to search out her gaze. "But I'm on pins and needles waiting to hear about this performance report that has put you so drastically behind."

Her gaze narrows. Maybe that was too much lava. "We'll continue when I'm ready. As for now, there are other things that are *far* more important than you."

She dismisses me, and I drift out to my desk in a disgruntled cloud. I replay her last words to me no fewer than thirty times in my head. Soon, I'm fighting tears and staring at my computer screen without having any idea what I'm doing.

And it's only ten a.m.

Thankfully, my work friend Lena comes into the office. She and I bond over books, and we're only now reaching that point where we might do things outside of work together. Realistically though, what we'll probably end up doing is sitting in each other's apartment and complain about the character arcs in *Game of Thrones,* like we do during lunchtime.

"Giiirl." She's got a folder in her arms, which is probably destined for me. She flops it onto my desktop, then presses her palms on either side of the folder. "How was that vacay?"

The sight of her round face and black bob is a relief, especially with all the emotions running rampant inside me. And dammit, Connor *still hasn't texted.* I swallow the tears and force myself to smile up at her. "It was amazing."

She snorts. "Yeah. I *bet* it was. Why didn't you tell me you were dating Connor?"

Her words stop me. "Uh...what?"

"That's what everyone's been talking about. That you two are an item." Her excited gaze bounces between me and Tamara's door further down the aisle. "So? Is it true?"

"I mean..." I twist around to look at the door in case it's open and Tamara is secretly filming this. I hate that I don't know the rules of what we've got going on here. Is it supposed to be a secret? Do I need to draft a memo? Who spills the beans first? I feel like I should confer with Connor before I say anything definitive, but I can trust Lena. "Yeah. We are."

She picks up the folder and slaps the side of my arm with it. "Seriously?"

"Yeah." God, it feels good to admit this. I can feel my chest swelling. "It just sorta...happened. I was going to tell you, but it's still so new." I swallow a knot in my throat. "How did you find out?"

"One of the other developers." Lena deals with all the departments, so she's usually got her pulse on the juiciest gossip. "I think he said Connor texted him about it or something. I couldn't believe it, so I thought I'd confirm with the source."

She flashes me a cheesy grin, but then the door to Tamara's office opens and Lena straightens. "We'll talk later," she whispers, and scurries off.

Tamara doesn't come out, just leaves her door cracked, and so I go back to email and compulsively checking my phone. Tamara pings me a moment later on the internal message client and asks me to make thirty copies of a handful of documents. She usually treats me like an underpaid assistant, but this is a particular kick in the face after my abysmal performance review. Like this is all I'm good for. Making copies. I sigh and get to work on it anyway.

When lunchtime rolls around, I'm officially on edge. Tamara hasn't finished my review, and Connor might very well be dead. I call his phone on my way to the lunchroom. It rings seven times and then clicks over to voicemail.

Anxiety turns my gut into a nut. Something is wrong, but I can't tell what.

I'm awaiting Tamara's next move like a patient awaiting a doctor's bad-news phone call. This can only end in relief or straight up cancer.

I grab a Caesar salad and an apple from the little deli in our corporate lunchroom. Just as I'm about to select a seat in the sunny, eggshell-white dining area, I spot Connor through the doorway.

His back faces the lunchroom, so he doesn't see me. But he's *here*, and he's *alive*, and my God *why won't that man text me back?*

My heart rate leaps, and I deposit my things on the nearest table before I hurry toward the doorway. I won't tackle him, per se, but I might whisper seductively about needing him to fuck me in the shower again since it's been more than twelve hours and we have a *schedule* to adhere to, dammit.

He's got his hands stuffed into his pockets and is drifting toward a small group of developers. Before I reach the hall, they walk off together. I'm left hanging out the doorway, my finger in the air, his name dangling on my lips.

*Almost.*

I go back to my lunch table and get out my phone.

*KINSLEY: Nice ass today. And every day. Yes, I'm creeping on you.*

I eat my Caesar salad, content for now, using up every second of my lunch break to read my daily selection of online magazine articles. When I get back to my desk, the internal message from Tamara is waiting for me. She's ready to continue the review.

It's now or never. Probably she was able to continue the review earlier, she just wanted to drag it out as a form of torture. She's like that. And even though that's speculation, it's also more than likely true. How many other bosses does this apply to?

On the short walk to her office, I'm struck with an idea.

An HR support group.

It goes off like a lightbulb in my head. Some sort of social media-based platform where HR affiliates could vent, complain, and seek support or advice. Maybe even *legal* advice, if it came to that. Because honestly, it's exactly what I need right now. Two weeks away has either opened my eyes or made my bad situation worse. I have nowhere to turn, because Tamara is who I should turn to.

And God help me, I want to see this idea through.

I knock on her door. She doesn't respond immediately. "Come in!"

I turn the knob and steel myself to enter her Bath & Body Works lair. She clears her throat as I step in, and before I shut the door I realize she's not alone.

Connor steps away from Tamara, looking startled. Like he's been caught.

Tamara is dabbing at the corners of her mouth. She shoos him off, sending him a coy grin. "Later, babe."

Connor glances at me so briefly, I'm not even sure he knows it's me. Because he hasn't given any acknowledgement. No recognition of the fact that we spent two weeks together holed up in Bayshore, cuddling in the mornings while he pressed kisses to my hairline and called me a sunbeam.

Not. A. Fucking. Word.

He breezes past me, and I twist to watch him go, confusion making a death swirl inside me.

"You can shut the door," Tamara prompts.

I'm moving in slow motion, robot style, and Tamara giggles again.

"Sorry. Got a little sidetracked." She smooths her hair, and I can't help but wonder what the actual fuck was happening in here before I walked in. My insides plummet to my feet in a disgusting slop. I'm suddenly so heavy, I can barely lift my head.

Tamara resumes the professional lashing—with more of a pep in her step this time. *What is going on here?*

Tamara's areas for improvement include my wardrobe, my demeanor, my professional disposition, my work ethic, and my timeliness. I wish she would ask me what areas *she* needs to improve on. I can feel the lava churning inside me. My gaze meets hers, and she has a weird smile on her face.

"So," she says, leaning over the desk like an acquaintance or something, "I never got to ask. How was your vacation?"

The question stuns me. I can't even speak. Her eyebrows lift as she awaits my response.

"Uh..." She's never asked me about my personal life before. Ever. "It was...well-needed. I mean, much-needed. Well-deserved. It was great."

"Seemed quite refreshing." Her tone suggests she doesn't mean a word of it. "At least based on the photos I saw."

I blink. "Photos?"

"Yeah. The ones Connor posted. They looked a little *suggestive*, but he assured me that you two are just friends." An icy smile pulls at her lips, and her gaze narrows. "Is that right?"

My heart is pounding now. I have no idea what's going on. And at this point, after being ignored for half a day, I'm less sure than ever that Bayshore really happened. "Yeah."

"Didn't you see the pictures he posted?"

I shake my head.

"Well...aren't you friends with him on Facebook?"

I nod.

"Hm." Her mouth turns downward, and she taps her fingernails against the desktop. Then she pulls out her phone and swipes idly at it for a few moments. "You might not have known, but Connor and I broke up four days before he left for Ohio." Her green eyes snap up to find mine, and I find a warning there. My whole body goes hot with foreboding. Because even though I haven't heard the whole story, I know enough of it.

At the bar the first night, Connor told me they'd broken up a while ago. I took that to mean weeks. Not *days*.

Somebody is lying to me, and for once, I don't think it's Tamara.

"I...I wasn't...I didn't know."

She shows me her phone screen suddenly. It's the picture that Connor snapped of him and I the day of the seagull uprising. It's plainly visible, a post on his wall. I blink dumbly for a few moments.

"Well, it's nice that two old hometown friends could reconnect over the death of his grandmother. I know she was so important to you." She pockets the phone, staring at me so intently I could wilt, but I stay strong. I feel like she's challenging me. Goading me with this uncharacteristic sympathy. "Connor said that it was important for you to attend the funeral, which is why you requested the time off."

Now I'm officially spinning in deep space, and I have no idea how to land. "Yeah."

Tamara wraps up the review and prints something for me to sign. The truth sizzles through me. The lava has turned into anger, and by the time I hit my desk, all the realizations have settled into place in the same way a meteorite crashes into the crust of the Earth.

First and foremost?

Connor is exactly the user my mother warned me about.

# CHAPTER TWENTY-FIVE

KINSLEY

I wouldn't say that I'm surprised when Connor doesn't respond to my messages that night, the next day, or even the following.

What happens instead is that all the carefully cultivated trust, relief, and joy that followed me around for two full weeks in Bayshore slides off like the top layer of pond scum. Gross and bubbling, all of those good feelings gurgle down into the sewer, where they belong.

And it's not like I'm jumping to conclusions here. No, I take my time to vet all the outstanding claims being made by the vile woman in control of my career. Connor's continued absence serves as the extraneous nails in the already-closed coffin.

Which means that I finally invite Lena over to my house. Instead of critiquing George R. R. Martin's masterpiece as I originally planned, I open a bottle of pinot grigio and lay out the Connor tale. As much as I'm willing to share, at least. I don't tell her the whole *pose as my girlfriend* part, but rather that we went back, fell in love the good old-fashioned way, and then he followed it up with a similarly old-fashioned spurning with immediate reversion to ex-girlfriend.

You know, like every handsome asshole ends up doing eventually.

She's aghast, as any good work friend would be, and she immediately offers to help investigate and, should it come to it, kick his ass.

We settle on Facebook. I pull up Connor's profile, and so does she. We compare timelines.

And there are no pictures of us. At all. Anywhere.

Even though I clearly saw the photographic evidence earlier that day in Tamara's hand. I think she's an evil bitch, but I don't think she's tech savvy enough to break into Connor's phone, steal a personal picture, and somehow ghost upload it to his own profile. The man is a tech genius, for God's sake. She can barely swipe on her phone with those nails.

Which leaves only one possible explanation. He purposefully hid that from me, and from everyone. Except Tamara.

The drunker I get, the deeper I dive into *why*. And it isn't pretty. Lena is as helpful as she can be, but the truth is, neither of us have any idea why men behave the way they do, and least of all why Connor is doing this. It turns into a drunken girl-power session, where Lena is undoing my braid and imploring me to dye my hair black like hers.

"We can have a girl band," she insists drunkenly, which actually makes me giggle for once.

"What will our name be?"

She hesitates for only a moment. "The Black-Hair Bitches!"

That gets another laugh out of me, which I'm grateful for. But it doesn't last long. A sigh ripples out of me.

"I hate being ghosted."

She frowns. "It's the worst. And I don't understand why these baby men can't have a direct conversation for once."

Her words echo through me that night, even after Lena catches a rideshare back to her apartment and I'm left alone and woozy, flipping through channels even though I don't want to watch TV. One hundred percent of my time is dedicated to not thinking about Connor, yet somehow, he's all that fills my mind.

And you know what I realize right before my head hits the pillow?

Connor didn't just want to use me to prove to his family that he had a girlfriend. He used me to make Tamara jealous. Which—I guess I'm all for that if it meant he would actually *stay with me*. But he didn't. He jumped ship the second our regular lives restarted on Monday.

Which meant that I was just a passing fancy. A hookup with a two-week timestamp on her forehead that everyone could see but me. Some vessel into which he could pump his false words and his unprotected dick as much as he wanted, knowing that I was lapping it up like the affection-hungry frumpster I am.

And yes. I cry.

I cry so much that night because it sucks, and it hurts, and I can't believe I'm back to this place.

Alone and unhappy in San Diego.

I take one full day to continue wallowing. By then it's Thursday, and I realize that I'm not cut out for being miserable like this. It's too taxing, and honestly, it's boring.

I'm sick of not living my best life. I'm sick of Tamara's ironclad manipulation and all the second-guessing about my looks and the pointless wondering of what a different job or man would be like.

So I throw myself into personal betterment. It begins with the HR pseudo-therapy group I conceived of. I start it on Facebook, slap a couple ground rules on the About page and stick to secret-inviting some of my HR pals I've made through the years and starting the discussion with clever memes and a few exemplary posts. On day one, it has ten members. Day two: fifty. Day three: two hundred. And by day four? It's pushing a thousand, and I need to enlist some HR buddies to help approve the requests to join.

I almost can't believe my eyes.

But clearly this is something my people need. Yes, I am delivering a service to *my people*. The handling of the group is fun. It's a great distraction from the sluggish monotony of my day job, and it's in this safe space I created that I begin to get more feedback on my own work situation. Most people implore me to quit and find a new HR position.

Someone named Carl says: "You are living in the worst-case scenario right now. What do you have to lose by quitting? It can only go up from here." Inspiring. Someone named Linda writes: "I would honestly stage a coup and throw that stupid bitch into a moat. Too bad we live in modern times." That comment demands the Love reaction.

Between diving headfirst into this sudden community I forged and hanging out with Lena more, days slip away from me. It doesn't take away the ache, but it at least drags my attention away from how much it hurts.

It's one week after I started the Facebook group that Lena brings up The Black-Haired Bitches for the billionth time. She is *serious* about this band. She has no idea how badly I sing, though.

"Would it appease you if I dyed my hair black?" I ask.

We're eating lunch together in the breakroom, and she nods so vehemently, I think her head might pop off.

"I don't know how I'd look with black hair," I say, holding out my wrists so she can inspect my complexion. "Look how pale I am."

"You are tan," she reminds me. "But..." She frowns down at my arm, "Yeah you're pretty German-based."

"Would you settle for one of those bayalage thingies?" I ask.

"Ohhh, *yes*. And, it's 'balayage'."

"Well, fat chance, because I'm not changing my hair." I smirk at her, so she crumples up her sandwich wrapper and throws it at me.

"Don't make me go find a black-hair bitch to replace you," she threatens jokingly.

"You can't. Because I was there during conception, which makes me a default Black-Hair Bitch for life, regardless of hair color," I inform her.

Lena goes quiet suddenly, and I can tell something is amiss around us. I look over my shoulder, and there he is. Connor. Striding through the lunchroom, dressed to impregnate in a slate-gray button-down with the sleeves rolled halfway up his forearms. His charcoal-gray slacks pair well with expensive-looking alligator shoes.

All the air goes out of me as every tender moment in Bayshore comes crashing back to me. But one rises above all the rest: when he told me his secret nickname for me, the night that we made love so passionately that it might haunt me for the rest of my life. He called me Sunny-kins. The sweetest thing that someone has ever uttered to me.

Was that a lie?

I whip back around to face Lena, unsure what to do. He probably jokes with the other developers about me. If rumors were swirling, Connor probably had to douse those flames. The slightest thought of what he might be saying about me causes mortification to drip through my veins. My cheeks flame, and I can't even remember what we were talking about.

I watch Lena's face; her eyes are following him across the room. I press my hands to my forehead like a visor and grimace, waiting for something. Anything.

"He's gone," she finally says.

I deflate, forehead dropping to the table. "Jesus, why is he so hot?"

"You can't think like that," she chides.

"It's impossible. You don't know what he looks like under those clothes."

"But he *ghosted you*."

I grunt into the tabletop. "I know." I let a few moments of silence go by. "But you don't understand how good the sex was."

"*Kinsley.*"

I lift my head, rubbing at my face. "I know, I know. I deserve better than that."

"Have you blocked him?"

I shake my head.

"Do it." Lena jerks her chin toward my phone. "Seriously. It'll make things easier. Block him everywhere."

I take a cleansing breath, feeling the fog lift. Lena has a point. Because I do deserve better than that. Like, way better.

Not just from Connor or whatever other love interest I might have in my life. But from myself.

That's what this whole week has been about. Reminding me of this. Pushing me into my discomfort zone.

And that starts with how I think of myself.

I deserve to love myself.

And I know where to begin.

# CHAPTER TWENTY-SIX

CONNOR

The first week back at work is easily the worst week of my life. Why?

Because I'm a weak-willed asshole who will do anything for career advancement. Not pussy. *A job.* I am pussy whipped by a career track. Which is why when Tamara shattered my post-Bayshore vibin' with her ultimatum, I only knew how to go with the flow. I only knew how to say *yes* to her demands.

She gave my app the green light. Which means she's getting her foot in the door at my dream company on my behalf.

I didn't expect her to do it. But when she called me on my way to work on Monday morning, my lips still tingling from kissing Kinsley's forehead goodbye, the path forward was clear. If I wanted the connection, I needed to play her game.

And her game involves staying the fuck away from Kinsley. The ultimatum was brutal. WeGo only happens if I eschew Tamara's hated underling. Even though that underling is the only bright sunbeam that commands my attention.

For the first few days, I told myself it didn't matter. We had a little hometown jaunt; who cares? It was nothing. It was a dalliance. Kinsley and I never had a conversation about what would come after, so this won't hurt anyone.

These are rationalizations I repeat to myself hourly during the first work week. I increase it to half-hourly at the start of the second week, and I don't find myself coping any better.

I miss Kinsley. That's the problem. I miss her laugh, her non-sequiturs, her braid, her periwinkle sparkle, her high-waisted jean shorts, her cotton-candy-pink toes, her fifty-pound stack of books that she took to Ohio. I even miss the dried drool that I'm pretty sure was hers from one of the nights that we snuggled without meaning to.

I would give anything for her to drool on me again.

I miss my *Sunny-kins.*

So by the middle of the second week of No Kinsley, I break down. I send her the latest text in all of follow-up history. I keep it simple.

*CONNOR: Can we talk?*

I'm not expecting her to respond, but I'm hopeful she will. But of course, she doesn't. Not that day, not the next, and not the next.

And I don't blame her.

Because even though she doesn't realize it yet, I chose money over her. I chose this undefined, uncertain chance at making twenty thousand more dollars per year over a soon-to-be-defined, way-more-certain happiness at her side.

The longer I languish without her, the more certain of this I am. Seeing her at work nearly cripples me. I go out of my way to avoid her, but when I do cross paths with her—like in the lunchroom or spotting her from across the foyer in the mornings—I stop breathing for what feels like five minutes. There's too much that I want to say.

And every time I imagine what those words might be, they all begin with: *I am the stupidest man on earth.*

*But Connor*, I remind myself, *your career is important. Financial security and prestige are the goals. Remember?* I can hear my dad's voice sometimes too, telling me that stability is the foundation of success. How will I find success if I don't have that stable, six-figure income?

I'm doing everything right, according to my father. He would have me drop "the Cabana girl" in a heartbeat if it means a chance to climb the corporate ladder ever higher.

A month ago, I would have agreed that dumping *anybody* in favor of career advancement would be a good idea.

Because progress is the goal, after all. More of it. Lots of it. All of it.

But now? I'm not so sure. I'm on my way to entering a higher tax bracket—just barely—but I can't remember what the point is. Not when I've got a gag order on all things Kinsley, and the only thing more unsavory than my cowardly about-face is the fact that Tamara's only goal is maintaining the illusion that she and I are an item.

I don't get it. And honestly, I don't want to know. Our six months of relative hell together proved to me that she's one shady mofo. But like Dad always said: every person can have a benefit to you. Even the least likely ones.

So that's clearly Tamara. She's the person I have to put up with to achieve the goal, which is a lead developer position at this ultra-competitive company. Tamara has her hands in a *lot* of pots, I've noticed. She's sort of like the dark web of Human Resources.

Which sucks horribly for Kinsley.

Aaand, I'm back to feeling like shit. On a whim, I call Grayson one evening when I'm contemplating drinking rum at five p.m. I should at least wait until six, but I'm ready to drown my sorrows *now*. He picks up on the third ring.

"Connor." His rich baritone sounds as crisp as if he were standing next to me, even though he's all the way back in Ohio.

"Gray." I sigh, sinking back into my couch. "I need some advice."

"What's up?"

I stare at the blank ceiling of my apartment. "You and Hazel are pretty serious now, right?"

A tiny laugh hefts out of him. "Yeah, I think that's a good way of putting it."

"Like, do you love her?"

"I've loved this woman for decades without even knowing it."

I nod. "Right. So, would you do anything for her?"

"Of course."

I nod harder. "Would you quit your job and start from scratch for her?"

He pauses. "Why?"

"It's a hypothetical."

"I'm trying to convince her to do that for *me*, actually. I want her to move to New York."

I sit up, surprised by this little tidbit. The early evening sun has lit up the western wall of windows in my apartment, and the rectangle of sunlight reaches my bare foot. "You mean leave Bayshore?"

"Yeah. She'll kill it in New York City. You have no idea."

I rub my forehead. Hazel leaving Bayshore seems unlikely, but that's besides the point. "Okay, but what if she asked *you* to drop everything and move to Bayshore?"

He sighs. "I don't think she would."

"But what if she did? And you guys had tried everything else and nothing worked but the only way for you to be with her was to move to Bayshore? Would you?"

Grayson's response is quiet, but it comes after a long pause. "I don't know." And then a moment later, "Of course I would."

I snap my fingers, but I'm not sure he can hear it. "Okay."

"What's all this about?"

"Just trying to figure out what the hell I'm doing with my life."

"Kinsley?"

"Yeah." I sink back into the couch, the claws of depression sinking in again. "I kind of fucked things up."

Gray grunts. "Is she giving you an ultimatum?"

"No." I gnaw on the inside of my lip for a moment, struggling to find the right words. "I'm giving myself one."

When Gray presses for more information, I don't go into details. I need to chew on this. But more than that, I need to prepare myself for the weekend. Saturday is the summer mixer for E-bid, which is like prom for adults except there are awards given out that don't contain the title king or queen.

It's actually fun, if you score enough of the tiny cakes. They go fast, so you have to be vigilant. This year, though, I'm not expecting it to be fun. Tamara will be like a fly buzzing around me, for starters. And I know that seeing Kinsley—if she even shows up—is going to be its own brand of torture.

All it takes it the slightest glance from her, and I'm taken back to our sticky vinyl lovemaking on her parents' boat. The times I fucked her so hard against the shower stall that Dom had to pound on the shared wall to get us to shut up. God help me if I think of the seagull picture *ever*.

It doesn't seem like a good idea to go, but I know I will. I've committed, and it's going to be my last hurrah with E-bid, even if Tamara and I are the only ones who know it.

Once I hang up with Gray, I remember the small package Mom had sent with me from home. My inheritance. Definitely not as large as the house Grayson inherited, five doors down from Mom and Dad's house. Honestly, I was a little disappointed to see the small box she handed over after the funeral. Not like I was expecting a house too. Part of me didn't want to delve back into the sentimentality of losing Grammy so soon, so I put it off. But now seems like the right time.

I tear into brown paper she covered the box with, and pull out the musty-smelling thing. It's antique, reinforced with metal edges. It's cool, at least, with all sorts of swirls painted on top that, if I look hard enough, turn out to be different animals.

Inside, there's a bunch of stuff. I paw through the contents. Metal clangs, papers shuffle. But one little box catches my attention first. I pop it open and find two gold rings inside. I turn them each over in my fingers a few times before I call Mom.

"Okay," I tell her once we've said our hellos. "What the hell are these rings inside the stuff Grammy Ethel left me?"

A long sigh escapes her. "You, my dear, have inherited their wedding rings."

The knowledge thuds through me. Somehow, that doesn't seem right. "But why?"

"Because that's what she decided to give you."

"I mean, why wasn't she buried with these? Isn't that a thing? I thought Grammy would want to be buried with the rings that she and Grandpa wore their whole lives."

Mom tuts. "No. She wanted the Daly family legacy of love to live on. So that the rings could be handed down throughout the generations." Mom pauses, and I wonder if she's getting emotional on the other end. "You certainly got the most valuable inheritance of them all."

I swallow a sudden lump in my throat, and I push the box away. "Okay. Well, I hope she's not disappointed in Heaven when I end up alone and miserable."

"Connor James Daly. Why do you say that?"

I fist the front of my hair. "Because I suck, and I value my career over everything else?

Mom sighs wearily. "Is this about *Kinsley*?"

"Yes, specifically, but I'm also preparing you for the sad truth. None of your sons will ever find love and happiness because we're money-obsessed tools."

"*Connor.*"

"You heard it when we were all home. It was a dick-swinging competition, except instead of dicks, it was bank accounts."

I can practically see her rubbing her forehead. This isn't how she wanted things to turn out, but here we are.

"I'm sure you will find someone else eventually," Mom says, her voice straining with sweetness.

"I don't want to. I already found the woman for me." I pick glumly at the wrapper on the bottle of bourbon.

"I want you to be happy, sweetie."

"Would you be happy for me even if it meant marrying 'the Cabana girl' with Grammy and Grandpa's rings?"

"Connor, don't rush into things. It's so early, still, and you don't have to—"

"Don't worry, Mom. I already told you I'm dying alone." Jesus, it must be great having five emotionally ridiculous boys for offspring. Times like these, I'm sure my mom thinks she's cursed or something. And I'm not even drunk. God help the person who hears what I spew when I get even a little tispy. "Besides, Kinsley and I could never get married if our own parents wouldn't show up to the ceremony."

Mom gets deathly quiet. The kind of quiet that tells me she's probably scowling or on the verge of tears, or both.

"Do you think we're all so childish?" she asks.

"Yes. You barely looked at Kinsley for two weeks while she stayed under your own roof. If that's not childish, I don't know what is. Kinsley is a ray of light. She's is fucking happiness and sunflowers and everything sweet and right in the world, wrapped in a lemur shirt."

Damn, it felt good to say that.

"Honey—"

"And she didn't deserve that from you, or from Dad, or from *me*." Now my throat is clamping shut, and I know it's time to go. This is the sign. Time to wallow in private.

"I know you're upset—"

"I should go, Mom. I'll talk to you later."

I end the call, feeling like a bigger douchebag than ever. Even bourbon doesn't appeal to me, so I put the glass away and head to the gym to distract myself with weightlifting and the indoor track. Once upon a time, Tamara and I used to come to this gym where she would interrupt my reps to get Instagram pictures. From the outside, we looked perfect. But on the inside, I was suffocating.

While I grunt and groan through my bench press reps, I think about what it might be like to come here with Kinsley. She'd probably be reading in the corner, her long legs dangling over the cushioned footrest of the thigh machine. I can imagine her getting so lost in the book that some big burly weightlifter needs to tell her to read somewhere else. Like maybe on the treadmill. The thought prompts a laugh to burst out of me, and I damn near drop the weights.

Need to focus.

No more imagining Kinsley reading in the weight room.

No more imagining Kinsley *at all*. Because if there is one thing I've fucked up in my life, it's the possibility of ever getting that woman in my arms again.

As I sweat my way through my set, one question dances inside my head like leaves on the breeze.

Was losing Kinsley worth the professional boost?

The bar clangs back onto the metal poles, and all the air exists my body in a whoosh.

I already know the answer.

# CHAPTER TWENTY-SEVEN

CONNOR

It's the evening of the summer mixer. I'm wearing a red bowtie with my black button-down, because #NerdLife, and I need something to brighten my days without my sunbeam in it.

I broke down and tried calling her yesterday, but the call couldn't be completed. I wonder if she changed her number. Which only makes me feel worse, thinking that my dick-headed absence upset her more than I bargained.

Tamara wants me to pick her up, but I insist on meeting her at the soiree. It's at this extremely nice restaurant downtown, with wood-paneled walls and crazy bear sculptures and an aquarium so large and appealing they had to put up a sign that says "Do Not Enter, *Please.*"

She's waiting for me inside the lobby, arranging the carefully curled waves of her hair over her right shoulder. She's beautiful in a way that is so tiring. She demands everyone notice how beautiful she is. That everyone react to it and feed into it. And I don't have the energy for that anymore.

I offer her a tight smile. "You look nice. I'm going to get drinks. What do you want?" Hopefully, this will fulfill the extent of my pseudo-boyfriend obligations for the evening. We don't kiss, we don't fuck, I'm not going back to her house. She knows all this. Still, she wants me at her side, and it's the last place I want to be.

"Chardonnay."

I nod and take off, waving at colleagues and clapping shoulders while I weave through the crowd toward the bar. I keep an eye out for those tiny cakes, because how can I not?

More than that, though, I'm looking for Kinsley. As much as I dread facing her disdain, I'm desperate to drink her in again. Aching for it. The infrequent glimpses of her silky braid at work aren't enough. I'm dying to pull her into a broom closet so I can ask her how she's been. What books she's read. Whether or not we can get our affection-o-meter back up to 3500 megahertz like it was in the beginning.

I'm tapping my fist against the bar top while I scan the area. There's Derek and Zara and Grant and Ulig. Most of accounting has gathered off to one side. I spot Lena, and anticipation prickles through me. Where there is Lena, there must also be Kinsley.

But she's nowhere to be found. The bartender practically has to slap me to get my attention. "What do you want?"

"Sorry. I'll take a Maker's Mark and a RumChata. I mean, chardonnay." I curse at myself internally.

"RumChata and chardonnay?" he repeats.

"No. Maker's and Chardonnay." Though I'd give anything to be ordering a RumChata for Kinsley right now.

He pours the drinks and hands them over. I weave through the crowds again to drop off Tamara's drink. She's by the aquarium, chatting with the CEO, Howard.

Tamara is one of the highest-ranking officers of E-bid, and she likes to make sure that she keeps rank. Which means that Tamara wants me on her arm because she wants to be associated with either my talents as a developer or my looks. I'm not sure which she values more.

And at this point, I don't care. I hand over the chardonnay, make some noise that resembles not wanting to intrude in their conversation, and walk away. It's a breath of fresh air—for now. I wander the periphery of the party, one hand stuffed in my pocket while I nurse my Maker's. I'm searching each face now. My preliminary Kinsley scan turned up nothing, so I must go deeper. She has to be here. Unless she isn't. And the not knowing is a special brand of torture.

But really, there are too many E-bid employees here to realistically see them all. Howard comes to the small podium they set up off to the side of aquarium, and the hundred or so of us congregate before him. I stare at the electric blue-finned fish zipping behind him as he talks about the integrity of our company culture.

Tamara sidles up to me a moment later. I glance down at her and sniff. God, her perfume sucks. It smells like high school mixed with cheap wine. She rubs at the small of my back, and I step away from her.

I can't wait for her link to WeGo to be completed. She gives me updates every few days, but the process is long with them. They require some barely legal level of talent, nepotism, and security clearance that apparently takes weeks to evaluate. We're still waiting on the confirmation of my first interview, but she says that at the start of next week I should have a firm date. It couldn't happen faster. And I wonder if she knows how fast I'll leave her behind once she gives me what I want.

She must know, which is why she's dragging this out. I know she's using me for something too, so it's tit for tat with us. I don't feel even a little bit bad. Especially for all the grief she's given Kinsley, who doesn't deserve an ounce of it.

And here I am, doling out more grief to Kinsley because I'm so focused on my career.

Applause swells around me, and I realize I have no idea what we're celebrating. Howard looks really proud about something, and then he gestures to the CFO to take the stage. I down the rest of my drink and head off to refill it.

It turns into a long evening. Each time a waiter brings around a tray of food, it's not the tiny cakes. Each time a long blonde-haired beauty approaches, it's not Kinsley. I'm ready to leave before dinner hits, but I slog through anyway.

Stroganoff, crab cakes, steamed asparagus, and lobster tails are among the options tonight. I dine mostly on Maker's and crab cakes, and then head to the dessert table to scope the options while plates are being cleared.

They've tucked the long dessert table off to the side, partially down a long hallway. The silky tablecloth swishes iridescent blue, which is E-bid's color. I tip more Maker's into my mouth, acknowledging the other dessert-friendly person creeping near the long table.

She's tall and lithe, with narrow shoulders and a tan that betrays a hint of a bikini line. Strawberry blonde hair hangs just below her chin, chopped at a precise flat angle. A wine-and-gold strappy dress clings to curves that remind me of Kinsley, and when she turns to me, my heart stops.

Periwinkle eyes sear through me.

I'm looking at Kinsley.

Except it's not her, not any Kinsley I've ever seen before. Her eyes are expertly lined with kohl and her lips glisten deep maroon. Her hair is straight—and *gone*. I must blink a thousand times as I try to understand what's going on.

"Where's your hair?" I finally ask.

"In the trash," she spits.

There's a storm brewing in her eyes. I clench my jaw and glance back out at the tables of diners. I turn back toward the desserts, measuring my words.

"I almost didn't recognize you."

"Good."

Silence pounds between us. This seems so pointless, but I have to try. "You never wrote back."

She purses her lips. "Was I supposed to?"

Between the different hair, the makeup, the elegant dress, and the jaded irritation, I don't even know this woman.

I shake my head, inspecting the ice cubes inside my tumbler. "I wouldn't have either. Trust me."

"You must have written to me *after* I blocked you," she says, crossing her arms over her chest. I get a whiff of her perfume, and I damn near crumple to my knees. Every inch of my body is alive again, like she's the secret amulet that brings me to life. "Which I didn't even do immediately. I waited a full week and a half for that. More than enough time for you to come forward and tell me it was all a horrible joke, but no."

I grit my teeth, drifting closer to her even though I shouldn't. She take a step back.

"I fucked up," I say in a low voice.

"Yeah, you did." She turns her head, and I get the sense that our conversation is over. But it can't be. I scan the table, wracking my brain for something to talk about that she might actually want to participate in.

"Did you get any of the tiny cakes?" I ask.

"No, they don't have them this year."

I scoff. "Are you fucking kidding me?"

"That's what I said."

God, the energy. Can she feel it? It's pulsing between us, and if things were only slightly different, we'd be cracking up about something already. That laughter is lurking, waiting for us in the shadows. If only we can get there.

It's the only place I want to get to.

"I'm going to find out who made them," I say, stepping closer again. She doesn't step away this time. "I'll order a special batch. Just for us."

Kinsley doesn't even blink. "I'll file that under 'More lies from a Daly man.'"

Her words irk me, but not as much as that acerbic tone. "You know, I can explain what happened."

"Well, I figured out you were done with me, so why bother getting the story?"

Irritation scorches through me, and I grab her by the elbow, bringing her closer to me. "I was never done with you. I was *compromised.*"

"Oh, I'm sure." From this close, I can see the gold shimmer at the corners of her eyes. The lush, dark mascara coating her lashes. She is a total bombshell. But still every bit Kinsley. I grit my teeth, fighting the urge to lean forward and kiss her. She rips her elbow out of my grip and stands a defiant few feet away. "You'll have to try harder than that if you want to explain yourself. I'm done giving you time and making up excuses for you. I'm fucking *done.*"

The sadness behind her anger nearly slices me in two. She balls her fists and looks like she's about to storm off, but I stand there, facing her, hoping that my presence will convince her to stay a little bit longer. I'd rather have her angry and hating me than not have her at all.

"I fucked up, and I want to tell you what happened," I say in a low, measured voice.

"No. I was a pawn in your stupid jealousy game, and I don't deal with *players.*" She practically hisses the word. "And on various fronts! You wanted to make your brothers jealous. You wanted to piss off your parents. And you wanted to piss off my boss." Her voice wavers slightly. "But you know what?" Her eyes are blazing blue and fearsome. "I was the stupid one. Because at the end of the day, I was the one who got played and mistook it for love."

# CHAPTER TWENTY-EIGHT

KINSLEY

There is a wrenching, gasping moment once I realize the L-word has flown out of my mouth. I had been doing so well—speaking my mind, being firm and honest but not too raw. And then I had to go and ruin it by telling my deepest truth.

That I fucking love this man and fell so hard for him that I cracked my skull on the pavement.

I would tug my hair out of my scalp, but I spent too much money to ruin it over a stupid man.

Connor's icy blue gaze hardens, as intense as a tractor beam. I'm shocked I've been able to speak around him at all. The two weeks and some odd days away from him have left me twitching and wanting. It doesn't help that he's dressed like the love child of a 1930s gentlemen and a millennial. Both strapping and dapper, his black button-down strains at his biceps, while that infuriating red bowtie makes me want to collapse into his arms.

It's not just sex withdrawal. No, it's the confusing mess of knowing someone's innards so well, you could sketch a diagram, and then realizing they've only shown you a carefully selected percentage of themselves. I can't tell how many more layers there are to peel back on this man. Or if the core is rotten and stinking altogether.

But deep down inside me, I feel like I'm not wrong about what we shared. That it meant something. That it still means something to him.

"Have you been able to forget about our nights in Bayshore?"

His voice comes out feather-soft, and that's when I realize he's stepped closer again. His breath hits the shell of my ear, and the shiver that dances through me is all the sign I need. I'm a goner. My eyes flutter shut, and I'm pushing onto tiptoes—because even all dolled up, I'm not wearing heels—to get closer to him. To his heat and the solid wall of him and all the best things I've been craving for the past two weeks.

I tip my head, hoping he might give me that which I'm too stubborn to ask for—his lips. His caress. Anything that is masculine and leather-scented and *him*.

"Have you?" he asks again, and this time his hand finds the dip of my waist. A low exhale shudders out of me, and I shake my head.

"Me neither." His head dips, and his lips find my ear lobe. My core tightens, but somehow I snap out of the reverie. I back away from him.

"Connor, stop it. This is horrible. How many times are you going to cheat on Tamara? First you start something with me mere days after you break up with her, and now you're trying to kiss me, while she's right over there? Not to mention, if you've been thinking of me *at all* while you have sex with her—"

Connor cups my face in his hands, his warm, rough palms sliding over my jawline. His gaze feels like a slap on the ass. "What are you talking about?"

"I'm not going to *do this* if you're with her."

"I'm not *with her*."

I scoff, trying to turn away from him. But I can't. He glances around and then backs me further down the hallway, past the edge of the dessert table. The chatter of the party disappears as we stumble backwards into the moodily lit recesses leading to the emergency exit.

"I haven't been with her since the end of May. We formally broke up a few days before you and I talked at the bar." He pauses, wetting his bottom lip. "But I was checked out of that relationship for months beforehand. We hadn't had sex in over a month. We were together, but in title only."

I scowl, but it's a defense against the effect his words are having. I don't want to believe him, but lord above, I do. Connor must sense the way this detail softens me, because he runs his lips against my cheekbone. Teasing me. Asking me for permission.

"Don't."

"Don't what?" He laces his fingers through mine, pressing soft kisses to my jawline.

"Don't fuck with me," I say weakly, but at this point, it's a formality. It's me, testing the last of my resistance before I give in completely and receive my bachelor's degree as the Connor whore I've always known I could become. Because apparently, he can use me, ghost me, *and* corner me at the company party, and I'll go along with it, no problem.

The bowtie makes it hard to say no. Among other things.

"I would never. Though I do plan to *fuck* you," he says, a smile curling his lips. He pins me against the wall with his hips, his hands squeezing their way up my thighs through the silky material of my dress. He grunts, looking down at my cleavage. "You look fucking stunning, Kinsley."

"Yeah, yeah."

"I'm serious." He searches my face. "You won't be upset when I ruin your lipstick?"

I giggle. "Come on. You know who you're talking to."

He grins and leans forward, his hot mouth finding mine. We launch into kisses so tender, so brutal, so unforgivingly hungry that I nearly choke on the urgency of needing *more*. It's like we've been away from each other for years instead of days.

His hands find the hem of my skirt once he hoists my thigh up. Soon, his rough palm is trailing a path up my calf, over my knee, and all the way to my panty line. When his fingers reach the strappy thong of tonight's underwear selection, he breaks the kiss. His lips are swollen and smeared with maroon. He peers beneath my dress.

"What's this?"

"My underwear...?"

He furrows his brow, nearly sticking his head under my dress. "Where are the granny panties?"

"I thought I'd mix it up. You know, with something actually feminine and sexy?"

He grunts, looking genuinely disappointed. "Is that why you cut your hair and did your makeup?"

"I wanted to look nice for once."

Connor's searching my face like he's concerned I'm not well. "You always look nice. Without all this stuff."

The vote of confidence is reassuring. It's at least nicer than him being relieved I finally look different.

"You are gorgeous," he whispers, then he presses his lips against mine again. "With or without the makeup and this sexy dress and the underwear that I really wish I could get a better look at."

I giggle as his hands disappear beneath my dress again, but then the real heat and hardness of his feelings make themselves known between my legs. He pulls my skirt up and over where our bodies join. From beneath the fabric of my dress, I can hear his belt clanking.

"You really want to do this right here?" I'm in disbelief.

"You don't?" He waits for my answer, hoisting me so that the tented fabric of his briefs slips into place against the scrap of fabric serving as my underwear tonight. I inhale sharply. Yes. This is what I've been missing. The leather undertones of his masculinity settling over me while that ice blue gaze pins me to my spot. Pins me to *him*.

It all happens in a flash. He pushes aside his underwear, then mine, and suddenly that slick and swollen cockhead pops into me. I gasp into the starched black fabric of his shirt, fisting the side until it comes untucked from his belt. Connor groans into the hollow of my neck, leaving a damp space there.

And oh, the magic of our naughtiness. There are fireworks and urgency and tension skating beneath my skin, creating this giddy recipe that has me grappling and begging to come within minutes. It's like I've never had him before. Like this is the last time I'll ever get him. Like he's the only one I'll ever want.

I cling to his neck while he makes powerful thrusts into my aching core. I want to scream his name until my voice rings through the restaurant, but even in this state I know that's a bad idea. Instead, I sink my teeth into the ridge of his shoulder, holding on for dear life as he pumps his hips against me.

"Kins," he murmurs into my ear. "Sunny-kins."

Dammit, he had to go and say that. The pet name sends me on a graceless catapult over the edge. I'm clawing and arching and burrowing into him, all at the same time, needing him deeper inside me than is humanly possible. He's coming too, with jerking abs and a stilted groan that fills my body. I press my head against the wall, chest heaving as I watch him for some sort of recognition of what the hell just happened.

He's disheveled. Broken. Scattered. He presses a kiss to my lips, then another, and then he pulls himself out of me and my feet slide to the floor until I'm standing on glass ankles and Jell-O thighs.

"Jesus Christ." He glances behind him while he hurriedly tucks in his shirt. We both work on erasing the evidence of the fuck-fest we just had in the emergency exit hallway. I adjust my underwear, smooth my skirt. I try to wipe the lipstick off his mouth while he laughs.

"Got a little carried away." The words remind me of something. The other day in Tamara's office when I walked in on the two of them. It reminds me of all the things I've been stewing over for the last two weeks. All the unresolved questions and lingering hurts.

I swallow a knot in my throat, unable to control the burble of sensitivity rising within me. He cracked me open with that orgasm, and here are the consequences. Messy, wild, and wounded.

"There's one thing in particular I don't understand," I say, my voice sounding strange to my own ears.

"What?"

"Why you would post our pictures to Facebook for only Tamara to see."

He pauses as he's tucking in his shirt, brows drawn together.

"I know that you did that. You shared our picture but made sure that only she got to see it." I sniff, reaching for my discarded purse. I fumble to get a hand mirror out so I can fix my lipstick. "I know you were using me. The whole time. I thought it was to prove to your family you had a girlfriend, but it was more than that. You used me like my mom warned me about."

Connor doesn't say anything but his gaze punctures me like a knife. And his silence is all I need to hear. It confirms what I know.

I'm right.

I wipe off some of the smeared lipstick before I store the hand mirror in my purse again.

"And you have nothing to say because I'm right," I say.

"We need to talk about this," Connor finally says. "About all of it."

I shake my head. "I don't think I want to."

"Kinsley."

People are beginning to swirl around the end of the dessert table. Nobody seems to have noticed us yet, but it's only a matter of time.

"You got what you needed from me, and I got what I needed from you." It hurts to even say the words, but I need to be strong. I was weak by letting him have me one last time, but going forward, I'm going to do better. Be wiser.

"Let me explain," he begins, but I brush past him.

"Do not follow me," I say in a low voice, so serious it scares even me. Now that the high of the sex is wearing off, shame and regret crash down around me. I can't believe I gave in like that. I can't believe I'd throw away my pride for one last fuck with Connor.

Connor is the type of cycle that's too easy to repeat and too hard to climb out of. I learned once. I can do better.

And if I don't walk away now, I never will.

# CHAPTER TWENTY-NINE

KINSLEY

I get to work on Monday still emotionally hungover from the party on Saturday. Walking away from Connor didn't feel good, but I needed to do it. I spent most of Sunday crying and doubting myself, so it's not like I came out ahead after our surprise public sex adventure.

No, if anything, making love to him one last time in the emergency exit hallway only reinforced how special our connection is. I don't know if I fully believe him; I just know that A.) the sex happened, and B.) I'm still as confused as ever about Connor.

It must be a full moon or something, because everything is a little off in the office. It seems like everyone who walks past me grimaces, for starters. Lena sends me a text as I breeze into the HR department: *Are you here???*

The air is taut. For once, Tamara is already there, her office door cracked just enough that I can hear her throaty hiss as she talks to someone on the phone. As I set my purse down and ready myself to sit, Tamara's voice cuts through the air, causing some of my coworkers to startle.

"Kinsley. Now."

That tone doesn't sound good. I silence the flutter in my gut that whispers the grimaces and the text from Lena and now *this* are all connected. Inside her office, Tamara is already seated behind her desk and looking at some papers. "Shut the door and sit down."

I do as she says, clearing my throat. I toss her a bright smile. "How was your weekend?"

She drags her gaze up to meet mine, and it nearly slices me in half. "Excellent. You're fired."

I blink a few times as I struggle to wrap my mind around her words. They don't make sense. Not even a little bit.

"Did you hear me?" she snaps.

"I...I don't understand."

"I've been giving you passes for too long. The list of grievances against you is a mile long, and enough is enough. You can pack up your desk immediately and vacate the premises within a half hour."

My mouth parts. "But...what grievances...I..."

"You are one of the most difficult generalists to work with. I consistently receive reports that you are awkward or inappropriate or showboating." Tamara lists names of our colleagues, and includes Connor, which feels like a low blow. "Your performance review was enough to warrant your termination, but since I'm nice, I gave you another chance. That ends today."

My head is swirling, but not because I'm upset. No, I can't piece together her version of my performance with my own lived experience. It's like she's using notes about somebody else and applying them to my file. She calls me Kinsley, though, so it's not like she's mistaking me with some other strawberry blonde in the office who used to have a long-ass braid and no longer does.

It's ridiculous. And there's never going to be a way forward with her. I feel that lava bubbling inside me, the same stuff that Connor helped me notice. I laugh. "Okay."

"You think this is funny."

"No, I think this is outrageous. But whatever." I sigh, pushing to my feet. "Is that all? Because I've got to go pack up my desk in the most awkward, inappropriate, and showboating fashion possible."

Tamara's eyes narrow to slits. "Go. You have a half hour."

I pull a face at her, which is childish. But at this point, I couldn't care less. I only hope it's as awkward, inappropriate, and showboating as she expects from me. I storm back to my desk and pull open all my drawers. When colleagues cast curious glances my way, I say, "I was fired."

A hushed ripple of shock rolls through the room. Everyone's eyes move to Tamara's door, which I left open in my haste. Nobody is bold enough to question further while she's listening.

I pack. And stew. And laugh like a crazy person. And continue packing.

Once my half hour is almost up, Tamara's heels *tip tap* out of her office. She crosses her arms, looking like some sort of modern office Disney witch. "Time."

I roll my eyes. I've filled my purse to the brim with the sundry objects and books I've kept in my desk space, along with personal pens, a stapler, my favorite paperclips, and post-it notes. I take desk readiness *seriously*, and hell if E-bid is going to inherit my fuchsia paperclips.

I take my leave without another word. And each step that carries me closer to the world outside sends a ripple of relief through me.

Finally. I'm gone.

And though I'm jobless in San Diego, which has always been the thing I'd been avoiding, I feel like I have more direction than ever before.

Tamara firing me was the biggest gift she could have given me. Now I just need to figure out how to run with the ball from here.

# CHAPTER THIRTY

CONNOR

Something is seriously amiss. The other developers are talking about some big showdown in HR, and every murmur of gossip sends my gut deeper into a knot.

Because somehow, I know it's related to Kinsley and me. I just know it.

It wasn't smart to have sex at the office mixer on Saturday, we both knew it. But dammit, passion doesn't abide by propriety or etiquette or sometimes even public decency. We were quiet about it, I reason. We kept to ourselves. It's not like anybody *saw*.

But still, I can't help but stick my nose where it doesn't belong. I rationalize that I'm going to Tamara's office to check in again about the WeGo interview, but really, I'm on the lookout for Kinsley. When I hit HR, she's nowhere to be seen. And her desk looks ransacked—drawers hanging open, computer turned off, and no sign of her ugly white cable knit sweater hanging on the back of the seat.

Something is *really* wrong.

I knock on Tamara's door, and she calls for me to enter. She doesn't look happy to see me, which is weird, because she usually at least pretends.

"Hey, how's it going—"

"Our deal is off."

Her words are delivered like a gun shot. The door clicks shut behind me. I check to make sure she hasn't blown open my chest cavity.

"Why?"

"The arrangement that you and I made specifically required you to stay away from Kinsley." Tamara is scowling so hard I think her mouth might slide off her face. "And since clearly you can't do that, then I don't think I can push through this interview for you."

My mouth falls open. "What in the actual hell?"

"I saw you two at the party. Real classy, by the way. You two are disgusting. I do like you, you know. Even though you've been an asshole, I've decided to let you keep your job."

Her words flow through my body in the same way as a logjam. She saw Kinsley and me fucking at the party. One mistake of many. But not the biggest mistake of them all. Not by a long shot.

My biggest mistake was partnering with Tamara in the first place. And I cannot believe that after all the push and pull of WeGo, after all this needless drama and harassment with Kinsley, she has the gall to act like she's doing me a favor.

"And what about Kinsley?" I finally force out.

"She's gone." She flicks her wrist like getting rid of a booger. "That was the first order of business today, and good riddance."

Her words make something hot and mean streak through me. I suddenly hate her so much that I could fucking tip her desk over and throw it out the window. Not because she broke the WeGo agreement.

Because she fired Kinsley for no good reason other than jealousy.

Jealousy that I inspired.

Which makes this all my fault.

"Good riddance, huh?" I sniff, propping my hands on my hips.

"Yeah. She's a fucking whacko. And so intolerably *awkward*." A scoff shoots past her lips. "You have no idea. You don't work with her day in and day out."

"I just spent two weeks with her in Ohio."

"Then you know."

"Oh, I do! I know she's beautiful. I know she's sweet and thoughtful and so *innocent* at the same time she's wise. I know she gets excited and jumbles up her words and something really wrong comes out which usually ends up being hilarious. I know she falls asleep while reading books in the sun and gets weird tan lines." Jesus, I could keep going for *days*. "She's not awkward. She's funny. There's a huge difference, but I wouldn't expect a humorless bitch like you to ever notice."

Tamara is watching me like I started speaking Hebrew.

"You didn't need to be so cruel to her," I go on. "She was trying to do a good job and be innovative and helpful. Instead, you made her feel like a piece of shit. Probably like you do to everyone in your department." I sniff again. I've started pacing the office, and I could put a fist through her wall and still not be sated. "Hell, probably the whole company. How many other guys are you stringing along like you do me? It's people like you who ruin it for the rest of us. Who use their power and decisions like some sort of shackle." Holy hell, if only there were a soundtrack to accompany this diatribe. It would be *intense*.

Tamara looks disgusted now. "Ugh. You've changed."

"Maybe you're right. I've changed so much that I don't want your shitty in with WeGo or this stupid power dynamic or even my fucking job." I pause, quivering on the brink of my next words until I feel that *shove* from within. "I quit. I'm done here. Good job driving away all the talent."

I turn on my heel and storm out of her office, the adrenaline vibrating so hard inside me, I feel like I could scream or puke or both at the same time. I can barely see as I weave through the halls back toward the developers' unit.

I stop at my direct boss's office to tell him the bad news, and with the way he watches me with wide eyes and parted lips, I probably look a little crazed.

But I'm over this. I've been unhappy for too long, waiting for some dream opportunity to materialize without putting in any of the work for it. And really, I credit Kinsley for this. Ever since I met her, the status quo doesn't feel right.

Maybe a month ago, I would have complied with Tamara and waited as long as she could string me along for the dream job that never was.

But now, with Kinsley's mark in my life? I'm sick of the underhanded shit, of the pandering, of the *using*. Kinsley's words come back to me, jarring and brash in my skull like they have been since she spat them at me on Saturday night.

*You used me like my Mom warned me about,* she said. And she's not wrong. I fucking used her. It seemed innocent, until it wasn't. Until I roped her into this bullshit. Until she lost her job.

I pack up my desk and do the same walk out of E-bid that Kinsley must have made earlier that day. I would go straight to her house and jump on her bed like Tom Cruise on Oprah's couch, except I doubt she'd even let me in.

Besides, I've got some shit to figure out.

The high lasts for about three days. That's how long I feel invincible and destined to find my next dream job on my own.

Except the job hunt reveals a lot of the same old shit. Same job, different place, slightly different number on my check. And while

I imagine continuing my career in every company ranging from Yahoo! to Uber, one question throbs inside me: Is this really what I want to do?

So I pivot. I hit up coworking spaces in the early morning and drink coffee next to my laptop and watch all the different entrepreneurs around me. Days melt away between networking and note-taking.

Soon, all the ideas that had idly occurred to me over the past few weeks and months are now clamoring for attention. I make a list of no fewer than ten potential start-up ideas. All of them involve what I do best—software engineering—but with a twist.

Now that E-bid doesn't dictate my days, I adjust to the rhythm of the coworking space. I shell out my weekly desk rental fee, adopt the other attendees as my colleagues, and shoot the shit at the water cooler.

I've been keeping my eye on a few industries over the years, so it's not like I don't have at least some idea of viable options for the future. But with the people I meet at my adopted office, I get the names of others who can help me.

The investors who might want to invest in a tech start-up.

The strategists who know how to whip up a business plan for software engineers turned entrepreneurs.

The local non-profits available to help steer people like me in the right direction.

I take my time. Do my research. And make sure I know as much as possible about this leap, now that I've found myself mid-air. It reminds me a little of Grayson back home, who dove headfirst into home renovations only to find out that he loved it. My hours of combing the internet for start-up strategies are the equivalent to his YouTube searches for how to deal with moldy basement tiles.

I've got savings that will ride me out for about a year, if I live frugally.

And thanks to Kinsley, I've got an idea for a new company that could change everything.

# CHAPTER THIRTY-ONE

KINSLEY

The first few weeks adrift in unemployment are so wild and unstructured that I feel like I'm living in a music video.

I am, partially, because I've been repeating the same sappy love song over and over while I recover from Connor. The ice cream I ate one morning for breakfast was just an experiment, though, and had nothing to do with a broken heart. Turns out, no ice cream before noon is a general rule I can get behind.

The sudden freedom is *titillating*. One Monday, I read the entire day and only leave bed for bathroom breaks. The next day, I spend at the library. The following day, I have a series of phone dates with all my best friends from school to catch them up on the goings-on.

And amidst all of this, I'm running my mega-HR social media group, which has officially passed the 5K membership mark.

I'm no dummy. I know I'm sitting on something that might really have a future. So I start throwing out ideas to the members. What do they want more of? What would they pay money for? What, for God's sake, will help us look past the struggles of our bosses or colleagues and allow us to enjoy our jobs again?

I start a website, which includes a blog, and the articles start pouring out of me. All that reading I've been doing for the past twenty-five years is coming in handy, because it turns out I have lots to say and a particular way of saying it.

I pump out roughly an article a day over three weeks. Some of them are wild hits—like *When To Call the HR Hotline Instead of Hiring a Hitman*—and others are just so-so. But the feedback pushes me further. I put together an e-book based on my best-performing articles and slap the stupidly low price of ninety-nine cents on it.

I sell five hundred copies the first day. And several hundred more per day from there on out.

So many copies that I can cover rent for a month with my one-dollar wunderkind.

It's a start, but it's definitely not enough. I need a job, and my hunt has admittedly gotten pushed to the side while I've been diving headfirst into HR therapy land.

Each time I navigate to the job search engine, I wonder about Connor. He's still blocked everywhere I can think of, but I sense that he's trying to get ahold of me. It's less Spidey senses and more common sense: he sent a postcard to my house of a cartoon sun. On the back, he simply wrote: *To Sunny-kins. I miss the lemur jammies. Can we go back to 3500 Mhz?*

I would have written back, but there's no return address. Still, I save the postcard. It gives me hope, in a strange way. Deep down, I want to believe that Connor is capable of being the man I believed he was. But in my own best interest, I *can't* believe that until he proves otherwise.

And I don't plan on giving him that chance until I prove to myself I can make the best out of my life here in San Diego.

Once I hit six weeks AE (After E-bid—not like I've noted the timeline in my planner or anything), a notification from the job-focused social media site, ConnectMe, pings on my laptop. I get notifications every so often from headhunters in my area who think I'm a great fit for their entry-level job du jour. I'm not expecting much, but I look into it.

The headline reads: *Tech Start-Up Seeking Talented HR Wizard.*

I smile, clicking into the message. A wizard. That sounds like it's up my alley. The start-up needs an HR head honcho and project manager. Some sort of creative wizard who can both handle responsibilities and go with the flow of a burgeoning business.

The posting is convincing. I check out as much as I can about the start-up, but their website lands on a generic *Welcome* page without any further information. There's no owner or director listed, and no reviews posted or even any products available yet.

Still. It's intriguing. And it sounds a helluva lot better than diving back into the same world as corporate E-bid.

I take a day to think about it, and then I respond to the hiring manager who reached out to me. Yes, I'd like an interview. They respond with a few suggested dates, and then we whittle down the times and locations. The interview is scheduled for that Wednesday at lunch at a trendy spot downtown.

Nervousness multiplies as time marches toward my first official interview AE. I wear my best business casual outfit to the interview, which is a sleeveless blouse with palm trees printed on it paired with high-waisted black slacks. If they're looking for a wizard, I'm sure the palm tree theme will help.

I arrive ten minutes early at La Solange, which is an outdoor café tucked behind wrought iron railings with a real live waterfall in the corner. It's full of other professionals and creatives on their lunch break or meeting for business. I don't have any idea who I'm looking for, other than I should ask the receptionist for a table reserved under the name WIZARD.

The receptionist smiles sweetly at me as she gathers up menus and leads me through the dense swath of tables and high-backed chairs. As I weave behind her, there's one head in particular I notice and can't look away from.

A man with sandy blond hair and broad shoulders that swell beneath the lines of his linen shirt. When he swings his head, an ice blue gaze meets mine for the briefest of moments.

And that's when I realize. Connor is here.

Of all the freaking places in the world.

He's at La Solange, laughing and acting casual in a business luncheon, while I am unemployed and skulking past in a palm-tree shirt.

My whole body goes rigid, and I struggle to keep my attention on the hostess as she leads me to my destination. When she pushes a menu into my hand, I slide onto the stool with a knot in my throat.

The past six weeks have not done as much as I'd hoped in the whole Getting Over Connor Department.

I peer over the top of my menu, eager to continue watching him secretly. He's halfway across the café, slightly facing me, looking even more handsome than I remember. And how is that fair? I thought memories were supposed to over-accentuate someone's beauty. Not pale in comparison.

But that's Connor Daly, I suppose, the dimpled surf boy who looks too damn good in a linen shirt and charcoal-gray slacks, both trendy and comfortably formal. His gaze swings toward me, which makes me gasp. I jerk the menu up to break our eye contact.

Because even though I'm desperate to drink in all things Connor, I can't let him know I'm curious. I'm supposed to be staying away from him. If I don't, we're liable to end up in that waterfall over there, half naked and screwing for the world to see.

"Kinsley."

His rough tenor makes me jolt so hard I drop the menu. He's in front of me. Right here. Right now. More handsome than I remembered and more masculine than I could fathom. Leather and spice reach me, and my hands tremble as I grope for my discarded menu. He picks it up off the table before I can.

And without my barrier, I'm forced to look at him. Because this close, my eyes can't do anything but find his. Those icy blue pools have ensnared me countless times. I steel myself, because one chance meeting with Connor does not mean I should be forgiving and forgetting.

But oh, when I get lost in his gaze, it's the only thing on my mind. The man is restrained heat, his body a terrain I knew like a cartographer once upon a time. Still would know, if given the chance to test the map I'd made in my mind. I swallow a lump in my throat, and eons stretch between us as we gobble each other up. My fingers twitch as I resist the urge to run my hand over the arc of his bicep, which is stupidly visible through his shirt.

"You dropped this," he finally says.

My eyes flutter shut. I don't care what he says. I just want to hear more of his voice. Because I've been deprived without it. I've been starving myself by keeping him out of my life.

And then he speaks again, his easygoing features hardening into something that I've never seen on him before.

"Kinsley...I made a mistake."

# CHAPTER THIRTY-TWO

CONNOR

My heart is pounding so hard that everything around me falls away. Except for Kinsley. Her strawberry blonde bob, the pink shimmer on her lips, the way her brows are drawn together in a look that says *what the fuck?* as much as it does *kiss me.*

Seeing her again throws everything out the window. I had my pitch planned out. The perfect opening line. The most gentleman-suave slide into the chair that had ever been seen.

But being here in front of her has reduced me to rubble. All I can do is drink her in.

She makes me forget that this is technically a business meeting.

"I can't talk right now," she finally says, her voice a low rasp. She looks past me, searching over my shoulder. "I'm waiting for someone."

"An interview."

She glares at me. "How do you know?"

I start my gentleman-suave slide into the chair, but it's wobbly now, and I clutch at the table for support. "I'm your interview."

She shakes her head, lips pursed. "Don't mess around. I'm not in the mood."

I gently set down the slim computer case I have in my hands, followed by the ribbon-wrapped box stacked on top. "I'm not messing around. I own the start-up that invited you here today. Co-own, actually. I've got a secret partner involved who hasn't been made aware of her status yet."

Her brows knit, and I realize that there is no elegant, pretty, or easy way of getting into all of this. I just need to start somewhere. Anywhere. I force myself to go on.

"The day you got fired was a wake-up call for me. I quit E-bid hours after Tamara let you go, because I knew that we both deserved more than we were getting. In all senses. So I've been making moves to create real success. No more depending on shitty people to come through when they feel it's convenient. I wanted to create something for me. For *us*."

She hardens at the use of that word. "You're shitting me."

I shake my head. I open my folders, pulling out the business plan for the start-up. This document is the result of all the blood, sweat, and tears at the coworking office. It's a perfectly polished ten-page document that exactly outlines what I'm gunning for.

"The company is Wizard Initiatives. It came up organically after I left E-bid. It's a tech solutions umbrella, which will house the various apps that are included in the ten-year plan. First and foremost being your brainchild"—I tap on the page she's peering at, which details the Risk Wizard—"the app that analyzes which risk realistically seems like the best one to take."

Kinsley drops the papers, looking up at me with an expression so raw, I am almost moved to tears. "Shut up."

"I don't want you to think that I'm using you for your ideas. Like I said in Bayshore, I took it as a challenge. But I'm giving credit where credit is due." I flip the plan to another page, where it outlines the copyright info. "You can see here, I've got you down as co-creator and partner. So, I mean, the job is yours if you want it. It made sense to me that you would handle the HR aspect, since that's your jam. But we can tweak those duties as you see fit."

Kinsley is watching me with watery eyes. She doesn't speak for a long time. When she finally does, her voice comes out a squeak. "What's in that box?"

"Our favorite tiny cakes." I push it toward her slightly. "I told you I would find out who made them. This is our special batch."

She scowls. "Are you serious?"

"I've never been more serious about anything in my life." I reach for her hands, because I can't *not* touch her right now. She doesn't pull away, and her small hands are engulfed in my grip. She's not wearing nail polish, which is typical, but suddenly I'm so curious to know about her toenails that I almost lose my train of thought.

"I want you in this, Kins," I say, squeezing her hands. "This way, we can carve out our own path together. There's nobody else I would rather have at my side. Every single thing Tamara slammed you for? Those are the qualities that I *want*. Because I want *you*."

Kinsley sniffs, blinking rapidly. "Oh my God."

"Please forgive me," I barrel on. The words need to come out before too much time goes by without her knowing how much I need her in my life. "I want another chance with you. And this time, I'm not going to fuck it up. You'll never doubt that you're the only one for me. And I mean that. I fell fast and hard for you, Kins. But I didn't realize that it meant forever until I tried to walk away from you."

The dampness in her eyes has spilled over now into full-fledged tears, which roll down her cheeks. Her emotion sparks my own tight chest and lumpy throat. Because everything that has happened since meeting her proves that I was wrong. Tamara and her link to WeGo wasn't the unexpected person I was looking for. Kinsley was. Along with the way she disrupted my life, my outlook, and my future.

I clear my throat as if it might help release its vice grip. "I'm overwhelming you, aren't I?"

"No, no. Not at all." She laughs, then dislodges her hand to swipe at one of her eyes. A tear has spilled. "I totally expected you to show up at my job interview and present me with a ready-made dream business and a sentimental confession. Not overwhelming at all."

"I've gotten a head start on the coding," I say, biting back a grin. "I can put your situation into the app first thing to see what it says about this."

"Oh," she shoots back. "My ex-fake lover signing me onto a business based on my offhand remark two months ago? I think it'll come back with a fifty-fifty split between 'run away' and '100 percent yes.'"

I laugh, squeezing her hands again. "So what's it gonna be?"

Her shoulders shake with a restrained sob, or laugh, or both. "You brought the cakes. Of course it's yes."

I surge forward, shooting up off my stool to come around the table and wrap her in my arms. She melts into my embrace, all laughter and sighs, and I bring my lips to the shell of her ear. Right where I know it turns her to goo.

"I love you, Kinsley Cabana." I move my lips down to her lobe, nipping gently. "These past six weeks away from you have been hell. Please, let's never do this again."

She buries her face in my neck, nodding and crying, and all I can do is hold her. There's so much emotion pouring out of her, and I'm the man to receive it. I want to be the guy who is always here to receive it, for as long as we can imagine.

"Luckily," she says, "this is one situation where I don't need the app to tell me the right choice." A few more tears spill down her cheeks as she presses her forehead to mine. "I love you too, Connor. Let's do this."

Our lips connect in their familiar way. Brutal. Tender. Heated.

We're at the beginning of our own epic love story.

And there's nobody else I would have at my side to write it.

# EPILOGUE



ONE YEAR LATER

KINSLEY

We're back in Bayshore for a number of reasons. First and fore-most, because we want to be. It's our one-year anniversary, and we felt like we should come back to the place where it all began. Not the after-work bar in San Diego, which is where our fake romance idea was conceived, but *Bayshore*, where our fake romance was enacted.

Except now, it's far from fake. It's the most real thing we've ever felt, touched, tasted, or dealt with.

We chose to celebrate that first day in Bayshore as our anniversary date, even though it was still a pretense at that point. We talked a lot about which date the anniversary should get—I'm talking hours and days and *weeks* rehashing this—and this is the formal conclusion.

Additionally, we've got a little interview scheduled with the *Bayshore Herald* while we're in town. They, along with everyone and their brother, has heard about our app that has, for all intents and purposes, *exploded*. It went viral three separate times, and I'm not even sure how that happened.

Point is, everyone knows about it, and now the *Herald* wants to feature us as the hometown heroes.

Which puts our parents in a beautiful position: dismayed by our continued relationship, yet so proud they could burst. But nobody dares say anything to us, because we've been together for a year, with no sign of quitting anytime soon.

"Is it here?" Connor pumps the brakes of the rental car as we crisscross the downtown streets, searching for the *Bayshore Herald* headquarters. I point out the petunia-lined front entrance.

"Right here. Wasn't this the old shoe store growing up?"

Connor grins as he eases into a parking spot. "I thought it looked familiar! We got kicked out of here once for fighting about whose shoe size was biggest."

I snort. Typical Daly brothers. "Didn't Dom win because he was the oldest and biggest?"

A mischievous grin crosses Connor's face. "That's what Dom was banking on. But it turns out I have the biggest foot in the Daly clan."

"And we know what that means." We shut our car doors, and I skip up to him, wrapping my arms around his neck.

"Biggest dick," he confirms, and then we share a long, sweet kiss.

"Ready for this victory interview?" I squeeze his ass before we hold hands and head for the front door. The past year has been a whirlwind, that's for sure. But every new twist and turn in our adventure only brings us deeper into love and commitment.

We didn't launch Wizard Initiatives with only one app on the docket. Once Connor found out about my side work in the HR world, we developed an app that catered specifically to HR professionals. In November, our Risk Wizard rolled out. And in February, the Hitman HR Wizard hit the market. Right around the time that we heard through the grapevine that Tamara had been formally dismissed from her position at E-bid after a slew of complaints were lodged against her in the wake of our departures from the company.

What a sweet, sweet cake topper to this amazing pastry of life.

Better yet, both apps are performing much stronger than we could have imagined or even planned for.

Which means that our business of two has now become a business of ten, and more expansion is on the horizon.

Connor brings the back of my hand, clasped in his, to his lips. "How does it feel to be one half of a power couple?"

I giggle as we push into the sunny lobby of the *Bayshore Herald*. "Are you preparing me for the interview?"

Our laughter fades as we step up to the receptionist and announce our business. She leads us into the bowels of the newspaper, where they've set up a featureless room for our interview. The journalist, a woman named June who graduated a few years ahead of us, is waiting for us with a big smile and a cameraman.

"So glad you could make it!" June guides us into the appropriate chairs while the cameraman tests his balances and whatnot. Once we're ready to chat and she's given an overview of what we'll be covering, the red light blinks, and we're filming.

The interview starts out normally enough. June introduces us, gives a basic overview of our Bayshore street cred (which classes we graduated in, which neighborhoods we grew up in), and then launches into our current professional work on the West Coast.

Except Connor gets nervous. Like, *way* nervous. He's rubbing his palms against his knees and keeps giving this fake little laugh that I've never heard before. I try not to stare at him while this strange, flustered version of him creeps out amid the questions. It almost makes me laugh, because over the past year, this is the *least* nerve-wracking thing we've done. We even appeared on a huge LA-based network. Hell, we've been in touch with Oprah's people already. *Oprah!* The *Bayshore Herald* is smalltime compared to the places we've been.

Connor gets his act together a little better, and we sail through conversation about our company's origin and what the future holds for our demographic. After a brief technical description of the Risk Wizard, June starts to wind down the interview. We went over the half hour mark but only a little bit, but I'm sure they can edit out plenty of nervous laughs in the beginning to fit the time slot.

"So," June says, turning to both of us with a big grin. "Have you used the app on yourselves? What do you think is the next big step in your lives?"

I'm ready to respond with something cheeky—grab a house before the property values skyrocket much higher—but Connor clears his throat, leaning forward to speak.

"I've been certain of the next big step in my life for a long time," he says, rummaging in his pocket for something. Something spikes in the air—not quite nervousness, but a sort of energy shift that make me sit a little taller and listen a little closer. I have *no idea* what he thinks his next step in life is, other than continuing to be my amazing boyfriend and business partner.

"Ironically, I didn't need technology to help me figure it out. My next step involves making this woman my wife," Connor says earnestly to June before turning to me. His words don't click for a moment. At first, I think he's talking about June, but that doesn't make sense. He wouldn't marry June. He doesn't even *know* her.

June coos and touches her chest, and that's when I realize that the red light on the camera is still blinking dully and Connor has brought out a small ring box with two rings sitting inside.

"Kinsley," he begins, sinking to one knee in front of me, and that's when his meaning crashes into me like a freight train. My jaw clatters to the ground, and I grip the armrest of my chair. Now it makes sense. His weird laughter and the way he's been darting around the apartment in San Diego like a thief sometimes. I've caught him tucking something into the bedside drawer a few times, and I always assumed it was a secret journal or something.

But no.

It's these wedding rings.

Because he wants to *marry me*.

"I've known you're the one for me since the beginning, when we were lost and pretending and struggling to find our happiness. But we realized that our happiness is created together. And I want us to be happy and sunny and together forever."

Tears are spilling out of my eyes even though I'm still not able to process this fully. Of course I'll marry this man. He's the only one I would ever consider forever with.

"These are my grandparents' rings. They chose not to be buried with them, because they wanted them to continue on in the Daly legacy of love."

That little tidbit really gets the tears flowing. Grammy Ethel's ring, of all things. Holy crap, I wasn't expecting this to happen. On camera, no less.

"I want us to create our own ever after, Sunny-kins. Will you marry me?"

I'm covering my mouth, looking at the gold band and sparkling diamond of the ring he's freed from the box. But I can barely see through the veil of tears. I'm blubbering as I try to speak, but finally I manage to force out, "Yes! Yes, of course I'll marry you."

Connor's hands shake as he pushes the ring onto my left hand. And then his arms are around me, pulling me into a warm, solid hug that as familiar as it is provocative.

Because that's how it is with Connor. He's my comfort zone laced with challenge. My soft landing edged with a push. He is everything sexy and warm and tender that I can no longer live without.

June is fanning her face when I pull away from Connor a few moments later. She smiles at us with teary eyes. "Congratulations, you two."

"Did you plan this with her?" I ask Connor.

He nods, and that's when I notice he's crying a little, too. He doesn't let go of me. I suspect he won't for the rest of our lives. "Yeah. I made sure she was okay with me proposing during the interview. How else could I get this filmed for posterity without you realizing?"

Another flood of emotion overwhelms me, and I bury my face in his chest. "How long have you been planning this?"

"Roughly six months."

I laugh, tipping my head back so my chin rests on his chest. "I love you, you know that?"

"I suspected." He grins, then dips down for another kiss. When we break apart, he brushes his thumb along my jawline. "You're the best thing that ever happened to me, Kins. You're my sunbeam. And I want to spend the rest of my life showing you how fucking awesome you are."

"Oh God." I squeeze my arms around his waist. "I think we broke the affection-o-Meter again."

"That means we surpassed 3500 megahertz."

"What broke?" June asks as she files away the folders she brought for the interview. The camera has stopped filming, so now Connor and I are officially lost in our own world. Murmuring sweet nothings and repeating inside jokes into eternity, which is what the rest of our lives will look like.

"Oh, nothing." Connor grins down at me. In a whisper, he adds, "We should probably go."

And the subtext is clear: *time to go celebrate.* Back to his parents' house, which is where we're staying again. Except this time, we're staying with my mom and dad, too, for half the time. Easing both families into the idea that this is a permanent thing, made even more serious by the on-screen proposal.

They aren't there 100 percent yet, but they'll get there.

I know they will.

Because if Connor and I could get *here*, then resolving our parents' drama will just take extra love.

And with Connor at my side, we've got plenty of that to spare.

Now I know the truth. Living truthfully, living creatively, living in love...they're all synonyms for *do the scary thing*.

And opening up to Connor was the scariest thing of all.

I'll keep doing it.

Because that's the only way to burrow even deeper into love. And I want to see just how far this adventure in love will take us.

THE END

**Ready for MORE Daly Brothers? Don't worry, there are still three brothers left. Next up? *Make Me Yours (http://books 2read.com/make-me-yours),* a grumpy/sunshine, matchmaker romance.**

**Need to circle back to book 1, *Make Me Lose* (http://books2 read.com/make-me-lose-el)? Read all about Grayson & Hazel's sizzling second chance/enemies-to-lovers romance before continuing on in the series.**

The Daly Brothers aren't the only brothers I write about! Check out the Fairchilds in my high-angst, high-steam billionaire romance series, The Bad Boys of Wall Street. It launches with book 1 (for FREE), The Price of a Promise (http://books2read.com/price-of-promise).

# START READING MAKE ME YOURS...

**CHAPTER ONE**

LONDON

"London, London, London."

Her name is Nancy, and the way she's saying my name suggests that she's either about to make a joke—and I promise you, I've probably heard it already—or she's very pleased with our first in-person meeting.

Since I've only been in this office with her for about ten minutes, I can't exactly tell. I barely know the woman, much less her tones. But I do know she loves purple, based on the infinite shades of lavender she has on her spiral-designed scrub top.

This is the final meeting in what I am absolutely, positively, persistently hopeful will be the last interview before I can stamp *NO LONGER UNEMPLOYED* on this chapter of my life.

She and I have been emailing back and forth in informal interviews for weeks while I packed up my apartment and left my life behind in Columbus, Ohio. This job opportunity appeared after I updated my profile on HireMe and waited with bated breath for an entire two weeks with absolutely no solid job leads here in Cleveland. Wait, scratch that. I've had plenty of job leads. But no job follow-through.

And I'm pretty sure I know why. It has everything to do with the fact that I'm the new girl in town. The new girl with an enormous, unsavory stain following her around. Like, you spilled wine on white carpet and *then* the dog shit on top of it. And then someone took a picture and put it on the internet, just to make sure everyone remembered *forever*.

"Nancy, Nancy, Nancy." I offer a smile, though I'm not sure what comes next. Nancy and I are technically pen pals, if that was still a thing in this day and age, based on all the emailing. I feel like she's my relatable aunt whom I've never spoken to my entire life until this one time I needed a favor. And she's going to hire me because *obviously*.

Or maybe this is just my wild positive self-talk trying to con the universe into giving me a steady paycheck again. *Please, Nancy and God, let me be hired by this doctor so that I can continue paying my bills and being a successful adult.*

"I have to say, if it were up to me, I'd hire you on the spot." Nancy grins, setting aside my resume, which I suspect she caresses each night before bed.

"I'd hire you right back," I tease, adding a playful wink. Dimples flash as she sends me a warm smile. Yes, we are definitely on our way to wine-buddies level. *Please, Nancy and God, let us be wine-buddies level.*

"But you know, there's one important last step." She folds her hands over the desk carefully. The smile droops a little. A cold breeze rolls in from somewhere, reminding me that we might not be wine-buddies level after all.

"Yes," I say, clutching my laptop-sized briefcase in my lap. This final step is the entire reason I'm here today. The final barrier between me and a potential big-ticket client that will pay my way through the next six months.

"You need to meet the doc," Nancy says simply, pushing back from the desk as if to suggest *it's out of my hands.* Her cinnamon-brown hair glints in the sunshine streaming into the office in the late-September morning. I can tell she's a looker when she's not scrubbed out and waiting for lunchtime to finally get here. The thin wisp of her eyebrow tells me all I need to know. This woman and I are more alike than she realizes.

And really? This is all part of my job. The job that Nancy knows I'd be great at.

The job that "Doc" has yet to hire me for.

"Let's go into his office," she says, standing.

I push onto wobbly legs, waiting for her to come around her desk and lead me to the plain black door nearby that says "DOCTOR DALY."

I'm hesitant to think this job is in the bag, even though Nancy and I are probably long-lost friends in-waiting. Even though Nancy contacted me herself because she was so impressed by my HireMe profile.

I'm hesitant because I've been smeared by my ex-boss, though that wasn't the only ex he qualifies as in my life. Nobody wants to touch me with a ten-foot pole, because that asshole knows everybody in the brand image industry. That's why I thought the medical field might be a surer bet. I've never worked with doctors before. Only politicians, tech start-ups, football players, and bumbling data geniuses. But people who could look at the pinky toe I stubbed three weeks ago and tell me whether or not I actually broke it?

Yes. Sign me up.

I can only pray that my ex-everything hasn't drained this playing field for me already.

Nancy leads me into the spacious and immaculate office of Dr. Daly. It smells faintly of cologne and latex, like a musky vetiver had sex with a doctor's glove. Nancy encourages me to sit in one of the two spartan chairs facing the expansive desk. She promises that the doctor will be in soon, and as soon as the door clicks shut behind her I snap into analysis mode.

*Dr. Daly.* I still don't know his full name, because this entire job offer is so hush-hush that she didn't even admit that she was in the medical industry until interview email number four. A lot of people don't like being associated with me, and I get it. It's sometimes uncool to admit that you work with a brand manager, much less a matchmaker. And I am proudly both. Sometimes one more than the other.

But God help me, I will manage your image, whether it's for the entire world or just one special lover.

I lean over Dr. Daly's desk, searching out some clues for who he might be. The building we're in is used by a hodge-podge of medical professionals, but I am most certainly in the cardiac unit. His desk yields no clues. A metallic cup of pens sits nearby, as well as a laptop cord waiting for the unit to return from wherever the doctor has carried it. The desk features no mementos. No heartwarming family pictures. No mess of folders or half-scribbled notes reminding him to *thaw turkey* or *buy more underwear—URGENT.*

This man has left no clues as to his brand or his potential match-ability. I frown, sitting back in my seat and tapping my finger against the armrest as I scan the rest of the office for more. The place is so pristine that I wouldn't be surprised if a carpet cleaning crew came in each night.

So the man values cleanliness. Probably he's a neatnik—which makes sense, given germs and his general involvement with health. Maybe even bordering on germaphobe? I'll have to make sure not to swipe at my nose or visibly pick a wedgie. Not that I'd ever do those things in front of a client; it's just better to know the hard nos prior to meeting someone. Definitely don't cough all over his face. Check.

But what else? I spot a few framed images on the far wall of the office, next to a tall, wooden wardrobe set off from another door that I can only assume is a closet or a secret, celebrity-doctor-only entrance to the operating room. I head over to the frames. Some showcase certifications. The largest one contains his degree.

*THE UNIVERSITY OF WASHINGTON has conferred upon DOMINIC DAMON DALY the degree of MEDICAL DOCTOR.*

Dominic Daly. I blink a few times, my gaze washing over the fancy script again as the words settle into me. The name is familiar. Too familiar.

Voices beyond the office door snag my attention, and I scurry back into the chair facing the desk. The door cracks open and I hear the rumble of bass, "Hang on." Practically a bark. It has to be Dr. Daly. Nancy comes into the room a moment later, her smile straining at the edges.

"Dr. Daly is almost ready to see you," she says. "He's still finishing up with a surgical consult, and it takes him a few moments to switch gears."

I understand what she's saying, but I can also see through her words to the real meaning. *He's a prima-donna who I need to handle with white gloves.* I've worked with everyone, on all rungs of the ladder. And this situation already smacks of white gloves and eggshells.

The door opens all the way behind her, and Dr. Daly strolls in. I'm not sure if it's a full three seconds or only a half second for me to drink him in and recognize who I'm dealing with. At any rate, it happens quick. This is what I'm trained to do. And my computer input is telling me the following:

This man is a fox.

This man is a dick.

And this man is too busy.

His neck is bent as he studies some files in his hands, barely watching where he's going, a laptop tucked under his other arm. He damn near barrels into Nancy, who leaps out of his way because that's probably what she has to do every day, like ballet rehearsal.

Nearly pitch-black hair is swept away from his face in soft waves, framing black eyebrows drawn together in doctor-grade focus as he brushes past me and behind the desk. I'm not sure that he knows I'm here. I'm not sure he cares.

But once the breeze of his wake settles, I catch the vetiver tang of his cologne, and something inside me clenches. It might be paired with the squareness of his shoulders or the fact that he stands six foot sexy in a white coat and a frown.

When he comes to a stop behind his desk, he sets the laptop down with a sigh. Icy blue eyes sweep up over me, igniting parts of my body that I didn't know existed. He could make my spleen feel erotically charged with that blue gaze shivering over it, and I wonder if his patients are getting turned on while under anesthesia.

But when his gaze settles on my face, something else courses through me. It's the thick sludge of recognition. Not just the veiled horror of seeing someone you know in the grocery store after ten years apart, but the dim recognition that you're suddenly in a very sticky situation.

I know this man. His presence connects with the name on the diploma in a final, thundering crack.

Dominic Daly. *Of course.*

This is a blast from my Bayshore past if I've ever seen one. An incredibly sexy, well-aged, super-hot-doc blast from the past. One that is currently scowling at me, his eyes doubling as daggers.

"You have to be kidding me," he spits, that whip gaze flinging past me, landing on Nancy. *I pray for you, my gal pal Nance.* "Is this a fucking joke?"

Nancy comes to the edge of the desk, much more confidently than I'd have imagined. This guy has probably been less than peachy to work with. "What are you talking about?"

"Her." Dom gestures toward me like I'm nothing. No, like I'm worse than nothing. Like unceremonious trash left on the curbside for six weeks. Like I'm the forgotten Tupperware in the way back of the third drawer, the place that people have been purposefully ignoring. "She won't work. Interview over."

I grit my teeth as I watch him press his fingertips against his desktop, leaning forward as though establishing dominance over my meek and seated frame. I straighten my back as I weigh my options. I wasn't expecting Dominic Daly to be the other side of the interview today, but I *definitely* wasn't expecting him to react like this.

He and I never had issues in high school. I can't imagine why he'd be treating me like this.

Unless my ex-everything got to him somehow. But that seems impossible. Like something from an exaggerated fever dream.

I don't have time to be treated like this. Not anymore. Not after what happened in Columbus. Not even if it means foregoing a five-figure payout for six short weeks of work.

"Great. Interview done." I hold Dominic's gaze as I come to my feet, making sure he can feel the razor edges of my gaze.

My only twinge of regret comes from seeing Nancy's devastated expression as I march past her.

# WANT TO KEEP READING?
Visit http://books2read.com/make-me-yours

# AUTHOR'S NOTE

The choppy waters of Lake Erie in the summertime are a special sort of haven, shrieking sea gulls and all. This series is set in a fictionalized mixture of my hometown and a neighboring town in northern Ohio. Writing this series has become a love song to my homeland.

Even though I grew up mostly critical of my little slice of the world (like most moody, dissatisfied teens—HA!), I now recognize it for what it is: a gorgeous spot in the Midwestern landscape, one that is capable of producing all the love and emotion and depth that a romance author could hope for.

I sincerely hope you enjoyed this visit to Bayshore...and I hope you'll continue this journey with the brothers of the Daly family!

# LET'S STAY CONNECTED!

Stay connected with me via my newsletter, where I share teasers, sales, and other exciting news. (Plus, if you haven't heard, I have an MMA romance series available, and **you'll get the prequel novella FOR FREE** when you sign up to my newsletter).

Or join my reader group, EMBER'S BLOSSOMS, to hang out up-close and personal! Early looks at new covers, exclusive access to ARC sign-ups, and more.

FACEBOOK
INSTAGRAM
GOODREADS
BOOKBUB
http://www.emberleighromance.com/

### *And before you go...*

Please consider leaving an honest review about this book! Even just a few words or a line mean so much to us authors.

# ALSO BY EMBER LEIGH

**THE BAD BOYS OF WALL STREET**
The Price of Revenge
The Price of Passion
The Price of Infamy
The Price of Forever

**WINTER HARBOR**
**(co-written with Whitley Cox)**
The Bastard Heir
The Asshole Heir
The Rebel Heir
The Matchmaking Heirs

**THE BAYSHORE SERIES**
Make Me Lose
Make Me Fall
Make Me Yours
Make Me Choose
Make Me Hot

Make Me Smile

**THE BREAKING SERIES**
Breaking the Rules
Changing the Game
Breaking the Sinner
Breaking the Habit
Breaking the Fall